It wasn't
love
at first

Shalini and I

It wasn't
love
at first

Shalini and I

Prashant Sharma

Srishti
PUBLISHERS & DISTRIBUTORS

Srishti Publishers & Distributors
Registered Office: N-16, C.R. Park
New Delhi – 110 019
Corporate Office: 212A, Peacock Lane
Shahpur Jat, New Delhi – 110 049
editorial@srishtipublishers.com

First published by Srishti Publishers & Distributors in 2012

Copyright © Prashant Sharma, 2012

2nd impression, 2012

ALL MAJOR CHARACTERS IN THIS NOVEL ARE 100% FICTITIOUS ANY RESEMBLANCE TO ANYONE LIVING, DEAD OR TO BE BORN IS PURELY COINCIDENTAL

Typeset in AGaramond 12pt. by Suresh Kumar Sharma at Srishti

ISBN 9789380349558

For the people who matter the most

Mithlesh Sharma
Dr. B.S.Sharma
Prabhat Sharma

This is for you!

And so is everything else..............

A quote which I happened to read:

It is silly to spend six months writing a novel when you can buy one for two dollars and ninety five cents.

Thank You!

Now that I have spent the time, a heartfelt thanks to Jayanta sir and the entire team for their faith in me and letting me experiment with the genres. This is my third book with them. A college story, an underworld story and now a love story.

Look forward to many more.

Thank you to all my readers. It is your appreciation which makes me want to write more. Do keep on sending in your messages, it's always a pleasure to read what you have to say.

A big thank you to all my friends, it is your presence which makes life so special.

Thank you to my family, for everything.

Prologue

She was in a dark green dress. She was fair, had a dimpled chin which gave a something special to her smile, long eyelashes, curly at the end, like a princess would want them, kajal around her eyes, kajal to keep away the bad omen from her beautiful face, a small parrot nose, which twitched when she frowned, and black flowing hair, which I would later know, she thought were brown.

It was Shalini.

2011

*T*here was a huge line at the security check as I heard the announcement for my name: *"This is the last call for RN Kapoor, I repeat, this is the last call for Mr. RN Kapoor on board Virgin Atlantic flight VS301 to London. "*

Damn, this was the opportunity I had waited for my whole life, a job in London, not only a job, a very high paying job and somehow I had managed to screw it up by partying all night and reaching late for my flight. That flight, which would take me away from all the confusions of this country and these relationships and the gym, the damn gym which had absolutely no effect on my body but had made my life living hell. Yes, this flight would take me away from the gym and into a country where life would have a meaning.

I struggled my way up the line, begging, pleading, coercing but somehow convincing everyone ahead of me that my time was more important than theirs. There was a pretty girl in the line, I almost stopped to say a 'hi' but controlled myself. She could wait, the way I had waited in this country, there would be lots of pretty girls in line for me when I landed in London.

I removed my shoes, took out my laptop and put it though the scanner. The security guy checked me as if he would actually find something. Bugger, they always let the terrorists go and held up the dreams of helpless people like me.

He checked me and said a 'thank you sir'. Rather polite for a Haryanvi in the Delhi international airport but then, this was the international terminal and I guess he had reserved his manners for the international people. People like me.

I heard the announcement again. The last call again. I ran my guts out and reached the terminal 1A. And in front of my eyes, was the Virgin Atlantic VS301 to which I had an economy ticket H58.

I looked at the plane, a Boeing something and I admired her beauty. Just then it began to move.

I panicked, I shouted but it seemed no one cared. No one cared that the flight took along with it my dreams of a better car, a better job, a better future, a hotter if not better girl. I looked at it, one arm stretched and the other holding my laptop, and gradually falling on my knees in slow motion.

The plane was now on its way to the runway and there I was watching it in pain through the glass doors. Just then it hit me, I had to get on that plane no matter what.

I got up, made my laptop bag a shield and ran. I ran into the glass walls, tearing them apart with the sheer power of my will. I had broken the windows and was now floating in the air, 30 metres above the ground. I put out my hand and an umbrella miraculously appeared in my hand, gliding me to safety. The plane was 500 metres ahead of me and was gaining in speed and was approaching the runaway. I looked behind, an entire battery of policemen was behind me but I could only see the plane. I got up, again in slow motion, and I ran.

I ran and I ran with my wavy hair flowing and the my shirt clinging on to my ripped muscles. I ran until the police cars behind me appeared like a speck of dust and the plane appeared like, well it appeared like a plane.

I had reached the rear tyres, the plane was on the runway and was accelerating and so was I. I overtook the rear tyres, and was now running parallel to the entrance when the girl who I bypassed in the security check opened the door, looked at me and smiled. She gave out her hand and I jumped. Miraculously, my umbrella turned into a flying disc and helped me get the elevation. The girl held her hand out. I reached out, held her hand.

But surprisingly, it was hairy. Just then I heard a chicken go

4

KukdooKuu and a slap came my way.

Hari: You jackass, leave my chest hair. My girlfriend really likes them.

Two things about that. One, the whole airport thing was a dream, I guess ou would have made that out by now, and the kukdookuu was my alarm. And two, Hari had no girlfriend, he had a wife. And also a kid.

I woke up, flustered. I ran a hand across my hair, which were not wavy. But they were still there and at my age and with my lineage, that really mattered. I had missed my plane, had missed the girl and had in fact missed a whole career in London. All I had to show for was an iPhone which I had purchased from Palika and a hairy friend who was no longer my roommate after his marriage but had taken permission from his wife to spend the night at my place. After all, I was getting married and having such night outs would not be really possible when both of us had nagging women at home.

I looked at my phone. It was 6:45 am. Time to get up and goto the gym and get into shape for my marriage pics. I looked at Hari. The jackass was already married. He could skip gym as much as he wanted.

Jackass.

I kicked him in retaliation of the slap which he had awarded me.

5

He groaned. I switched on the light, he took my pillow and covered his eyes. He was not getting up for atleast 2 more hours, and would then leave for home. And I had to make the journey, the long journey to the gym, even on a Saturday. I rubbed my eyes, yawned and tried to look forward to the day but failed miserably. I felt my body to see if the gym sessions had made any affect. Again, no ripped muscles, just a little paunch which was growing by the day.

I then thought about my dream. In all my dreams, I addressed myself as RN Kapoor. My name was not RN Kapoor, it was nowhere close to RN Kapoor.

I groaned, picked up the magazine section of the newspaper, that always made me smile, and went into the toilet to get ready for what was going to be another battle. Battle as I had maggi last night and that did not go well with my bowel movements.

I sat in there for half an hour, reading about all the gossip about what one girl, atleast five years younger than me, had to say about same sex marriages. Then I read about a boy, five years younger than that girl, and how he had again managed to sell out Madisson Square Garden within five minutes of tickets going on sale. This was news which I really did not care about, but the newspaper magazine printed it, put really hot girls photos along with it, and hence I read it. I switched to the cartoon section, read what Archie and the gang were upto and then browsed through the page three hoping that none of my friends were there in it.

They never were, but still I checked.

But nothing happened on the toilet front so I got up. I would go again in the gym, that would help me pass time. Kriti only took note of how much time I spent there, not what I did. I smiled at the thought and brushed my teeth and I then lay on my bed again.

I heard the same irritating tone of the alarm. I tried to ignore it but I knew that the alarm would win the battle- as it had for the last infinite years. I put it on snooze and slept for five more minutes.

The alarm tone went off again. It was 7:20 am. Even though it was a Saturday and it was off at office, I still had to getup. I had gained 10 kgs in the last one year and if things continued going the way they were, a heart problem was just around the corner. That is the problem with these managerial jobs, you just sit and stare into the computer, and the size of the computer keeps on getting smaller, but the size of your belly keeps on increasing. Maybe Kriti was right in forcing me to the gym.

Unwittingly I got up and went into the shower. I looked at myself in the mirror. I still looked young. I was 30 but could any day pass for 29 and a half. I still had the typical Indian skin color, no matter how many fairness cream tubes I had emptied on my face- my skin was the same wheatish brown it had been since birth, my height was the five feet something, I had for all reasons stopped growing after 16, but I was 80 kgs now instead of the 60 I had been some years ago and the 50 kgs I had been when I was 16. It seemed as if all the fat had gone into my belly. The rest of me was fine, it was only the belly which was protruding. And I did not even drink a lot of beer. Still, the belly looked swollen as if I were pregnant. I played around with it a little, it was jiggly. Some would find it cute, I found it fun, but not Kriti. She hated it.

The belly had ensured that I could not wear t shirts anymore so even when I was going to the gym, I put on a shirt.

A loose shirt. Most of my hair were still there, they had started receding but it was not time for alarm bells yet. Plus, the good thing was that they were not everywhere. I had a pretty clean back so that was good. The color of the hair was also fine. Some greys, but not enough to warrant usage of hair color. I put on my spectacles, a rimless frame with thin lens, another recent addition to my body and looked at myself. I looked fairly presentable if not overtly handsome. This thought, every day, made me want to skip gym but Kriti, my fiancé, had told me that I had to get in shape before the marriage. Her logic was that marriage photographs were clicked only once in life and I had to look good in them for her sake.

So I made the effort. Not that I had any choice.

The phone rang. It was her, she called me every morning at 7:30 to ensure that I had got up and was on my way to lose weight. She was always sleeping at that time but that was besides the point. We said our good mornings, she in a groggy voice and me trying to be as cheerful as a guy forsaking his sleep to give pain to his own body by lifting weights can. I put on my shoes, plugged in my iPod, gave Hari a disgusting look, he would be gone by the time I got back, got into my car and took the road towards the gym which was around 5 kms.

On the way I wondered where life was taking me. The early days of job seemed like only yesterday. There was no longer any getting

9

up and not remembering how I reached home, there was no sleeping till noon on weekends, and there was definitely no running away from commitment anymore. Life had come a full circle. I was 30 years old, had completed post graduation- MBA, from a tier one business school, was at a good managerial level at work, was making good money and was engaged to get married to a girl of my parent's choice. Not that I could complain. I was too scared to ask any girl I had dated to marry me, and no matter how young I looked (twenty nine and a half), age was no longer on my side. If I did not get married now, there could be problems finding me a bride later on in life.

A nice Saturday evening now meant ordering in from a restaurant, having a couple of beers with friends, and talking about the share market movement along with the usual topic that all guys have- girls. The same old conversations which we used to have even at 25, but they seemed a lot more fun back then.

Work meanwhile was still in Delhi. After completing post grad, my parents had finally agreed to leave the small town and come and live with me. But they could not adjust to the life of the city. I used to leave at 8 and come back at around the same time at night. My parents knew nobody in the city and at that age, it is difficult to make new friends, so they decided to move back. So I was again alone in the city with some friends and colleagues for company.

Hari, my only real friend who I had known for 13 years now, had decided that he had studied enough and did not try for post graduation. He continued working and got married at 27. At 29 he had a kid, a baby boy who luckily took to his wife and not him. Hari became busy with the usual chores of life and we used to meet less often, but the friendship was as good as ever. I remembered it was his kid's birthday soon and I had to buy him something. I noted it on my notepad which always stayed in my car. The drive was 5 km but even in the empty morning roads, I ensured that it took me atleast 25 minutes.

I reached the gym and went straight to the treadmill. The gym had the usual crowd at this time. There would be old people who would sweat it out for around an hour on the treadmill, then there would be people in their early twenties who would be drinking protein shakes and lifting weights which people with their body structure should not be lifting. And there would be the ladies who all the gym trainers would try and impress, and at times succeed. And there would be people like me, who had still not given up hope of having a six pack yet, but knew their limitations and hence divided their time between all exercises.

I said the usual hellos and started my one hour work out session. The gym would be the only 'me' time I had during the day as the rest of it was to be spent on shopping for my marriage. I extended the

11

session by fifteen minutes, obviously not because I liked exercise, and took a long cold shower. I changed and called Kriti telling her that I would pick her in fifteen minutes from her place. We would then head to my place for breakfast and then have a marathon of a shopping day. Not fun, I know, but wait till you have a fiancé and an impending marriage.

I put on a jeans and a shirt and looked at my belly. After one hour and fifteen minutes of workout it was still jiggly. I played with it a little, smiled, tucked in the shirt, got back into the car and reached Kriti's apartment.

Kriti shared her apartment with one other girl and both of them hated each other. So Kriti always looked for a chance to get out of her house and into mine. She said she did that because she loved me and at times I also thought that was the actual reason. But love was too strong a word. Love is too strong a word, and a word which is overly used.

I parked the car at the gate of her colony and called her again. "Kriti dear, am there."

"Honey, it will take me just five minutes. I hope you don't mind."

I didn't know why it always took her five minutes. I had called her 30 minutes ago and at that time, she said she was perfectly ready. She just had to put on make up. But now again, she said it would take five more minutes. Five minutes were still fine, but her five minutes always meant fifteen. I had not brought forward the point of her never being on time and I used to always smile when she came. But I had decided that today I would atleast mention it that I did not like waiting alone in the car.

I pulled back the driver seat, and tried to sleep. Five minutes passed by, then fifteen, then thirty. I could not sleep. I did not know what she was doing up there. I had called her a couple of times in between but she did not receive the calls. I was about to getup and goto her place when I saw her running down the stairs. I pulled up the seat and was ready to give her a piece of my mind, but then I saw her and the testosterone part of me took over.

She was wearing very casual clothes, a yellow top and a blue jeans teemed with a scarf, but she was looking out of this world pretty. She was fair, very fair, had shoulder length hair, a small pointed nose, rosy lips and cheeks and a small dimple on both sides. She was five feet four, was a little plump, not fat, just the right plump an Indian girl is and had an angelic look to her. I was mesmerised every time I saw her and I thanked my parents silently in my head. They were the ones who had introduced me to her in the first place.

She opened the car door "Sorry honey, it took me a little more time than what I had said. Hope you don't mind."

I had a goofy smile on my face. "Mind, not at all. In fact, I took a little nap as I was tired from the gym." I chickened out of shouting at her for being late- well, obviously, she was so pretty.

She sat down and gave me a little peck on the cheek. "Good boy. Am so proud you went to the gym."

I was being treated like a dog but I did not really mind. She was just so pretty. The dog patting got a smile on my face and we headed back to my place.

Kriti was an architect by profession. So basically, I did not understand her work. She had been a typical Delhi girl who studied in one of the DPS schools, which I hear also have a branch in Nepal but again, that is besides the point. After her class 12 got completed, parents had moved to Chandigarh but she went to architecture school in Delhi and had been working for the last two years after passing out from there.

And there in lied our biggest difference.

She was 25, I was 30. It seemed as if she was from another planet altogether. Right now, she was in the phase of the weekday parties, the binge drinking, the dancing, the movie marathons and all the other things you expect from a typical 25 year old Delhi girl. And I had already been through that phase and reliving it did not seem to be that great an idea. Plus, all her friends were also 25 and I felt so out of place when we met them. They looked like little kids drooling over Shah Rukh Khan and trying to tease me to make me uncomfortable. It used to be weird in front of her friends. Once I kissed her by mistake in front of them, that too a normal peck on the cheek, and I had to hear about that for the next 20 days on all sorts of platforms.

I had met Kriti through an online portal. As soon as I crossed 29, my parents got sick worried about my marriage. They kept on asking me whether I had already found someone. They said they would not be happy about it but would still accept and get me married to her. I did have some female friends, but the last real relationship I had was with Pooja who had left me for her ex fiancé. After that there had been some minor flirtations, some steady dates, but no one marriage material. Or maybe, none of the girls who I went out with found me marriage material. Whatever the case, I was 30, earning well, not bad to look at and unmarried.

The last part became a huge cause of concern for my parents.

My parents, even though completely computer illiterate, had managed to create a profile for me on one of those marriage sites. They even uploaded a nice photo of me and made me look like the most eligible bachelor in the profile. I don't know how they managed it, but I think they used photoshop and all to make me look more fair. What those tubes of fairness creams could not manage in a decade was done in ten minutes by the computer.

I got approached by quite a few people and ended up meeting around 4 girls before Kriti came into the picture. I just saw her and said yes. It was not that I would get to know any of the girls by just meeting them for a few times, and I was sure I would never get anyone as pretty as Kriti. It was not love at first sight or anything of that sort. It was just that she was so beautiful. So I had said yes.

My parents had then come over to Delhi and had met with her parents. I still remember she was wearing a red kurta the day my parents had come to visit. She was looking so pretty that it was impossible to say no to her. The marriage was finalised, but was fixed for a date 8 months ahead as there was no mahurat till then. Four out of the eight months had passed. We also got time to know each other.

She was a nice girl. The more I got to know her, the more I thought she had a very pure heart. But she was a typical 'girl' girl. The sort who will not step out if they had a bad hair day, who would admire themselves in a mirror wherever they saw one, who would take hours to get ready for a ten minute coffee. And, she was 25.

We had gotten close over the last four months and were now practically boyfriend and girlfriend and practically lived together. Half of her things were already at my apartment and it was only a matter of time before the other half also shifted. Most of the times, I enjoyed her company as she had the energy of youth with her, but at other times, I just wanted to be left alone.

16

Left alone to sleep, to think, to do nothing. And that is what she never understood. We reached home and climbed the stairs to my apartment. She already had a key and opened the door. She had promised to make me an Indian breakfast today and I was kind of looking forward to it but as soon as she entered she said "Honey, I have just manicured my hands yesterday and do not want to spoil my nails."

She showed me her nails. They did look pretty and should not have been used to make parathas. "Could you just make bread and eggs and we can have the aaloo parathas next week." She fluttered her eyes as she spoke. No one could say no to the fluttering eyes.

I just wondered for how long.

I went to the kitchen, cracked open the eggs and made the omelette.

I was a pretty decent cook. Living alone teaches you that. The rest of the day passed in a similar tone. There was lots of eye fluttering and lots of waiting. In the car, in the saree shops, in the jewellery shops, in the lehenga shops, in the shoe shops, and even in the shops which sold jeans which had nothing to do with the marriage. And there were no aaloo parathas.

She liked Italian food so we had lunch at a pizzeria and she felt that both of us had too much for lunch and were gaining weight which was not good before our marriage, so we had a salad at Subway for dinner. I hated Italian and I hated subway and I hated salad more than both of them put together.

And it was not that I even loved her. But it was that she was too damn beautiful. I again wondered in how much time would I get immune to her beauty. One thing was for sure, it was not happening today.

We reached back home at around 11 pm and she decided to stay on at my place because if she went home, she would get into a fight with her roommate and that would upset her. But even when she stayed over, nothing much happened.

We were getting married in 4 months and she said that I should wait as it was just four months. So instead of doing what a young couple alone in a room should do, she made me watch movies. I seriously did not have the energy to watch movies, and that too romantic bad movies, and that too in English.

Plus, there were no aaloo parathas. I felt hungry. A Subway salad did nothing to me. So we saw a movie and slept around 2. 'The Notebook' I think it was called. A senti movie about two lovers.

Honestly, I actually kind of liked it and was happy that atleast our choices weren't that different. But at the end of the movie she declared that it was the worst she had ever seen. I again, just nodded in agreement. We finally got into bed to sleep. No action, just sleep.

The good thing was that the gym was closed on a Sunday and I could sleep till 9.

This was the first time we had slept on the same bed. Nothing had happened but it was atleast a step in the right direction.

Even though it was a Sunday and I had the liberty to sleep till nine, for some good reason, I gotup at 7 again. No alarm, just gotup. I hated early mornings. I looked around and I realised that Kriti was also there. I looked at her, she looked like the best thing that had ever happened to my bed, or even the best thing that had ever happened to me.

She had changed into cute little yellow polka dotted pyjamas with a matching yellow polka dotted tshirt. Her hair were open and were all over her face. Her lips were apple red and she was the most beautiful girl I had ever seen.

Just then her eyes opened. Beautiful black big eyes. And the best part was that I could see the love in them. The love I had not seen in any girl's eyes for me for a very long time. I thanked the matrimonial site once more and I was sure that I was doing the right thing by marrying her.

"Darling, will you like your morning breakfast on bed?" I said that, not she.

She smiled. A lazy sleepy pretty smile, and nodded. I gotup to make the eggs with juice and bread. I actually had a smile on my face while cracking open the egg.

The rest of the day was similar to the last one. She was still as beautiful and there was as much waiting with the Italian food for lunch and salad for dinner. She decided to goto her apartment for the night as her office cab would pick her from there. I dropped her off and got back after a long weekend with not much productivity for me, ready for another five days at work.

There are some things that do not change no matter at what level you are at work. You still have someone to report to, you still have deadlines which cannot be met, you still feel that the year end increments are not high enough, you still feel that you and not your colleague deserve the promotion, you still feel that some other job would pay you much more for what you are doing, you still have a bunch of people who start off as office colleagues and then become friends, you still have a bunch of people who start as friends and then become colleagues, and you still have the long cigarette breaks where you vent out all the frustration, even if you don't really smoke.

My office was no different. I no longer worked as an engineer. In fact, I now worked in the marketing and distribution channel for one of the big FMCG companies which used to sell all kinds of things. I was responsible for one particular brand. My work, like most other jobs, was monotonous for the most part wherein there is a set system and you just have to fit in. But there were chances when you got to show your creative ability and that was the part which kept me, and millions of other people like me going. Plus, the money was good, and money was needed to pay the bills, and with the impending marriage, it was also needed to pay for the honeymoon, the new furniture, the new wardrobe, the new house etc.

I was pretty satisfied with my job. I had been in this job for almost 3 years now, right after finishing MBA. There were some office flirtations and some sort of flings in the beginning when everyone is new to work and do not really know what to do. But that had now settled and I fit into the office like old furniture. I used to hit the gym after office hours, or at times in the morning, for my marriage and then used to go back home, cook some light food, watch some television, chat on the phone with Kriti for some time and then goto sleep. A usual boring routine followed by every office goer who has a fiancé or a girlfriend. For the (un)lucky few who don't, the talking on the phone part is replaced by watching more television or drinking beer. But at the end it's all the same. You get used to it and it stops making a difference.

In my case the 'chat for sometime on the phone' had recently started becoming 'chat for a hell lot of time' on the phone. Kriti had so much to tell about office. Either that her office was too happening or that she just liked talking too much. She would tell me everything that happened in her day. She would reach office late every day- she needed some extra time to get ready, and then she would try and confuse her manager and make him believe that she was indeed on time. She said he would agree but I knew he had a similar problem like me, he could not say anything to those fluttering eyelashes. She would then login to her computer and check the first mails of the day. She would then have breakfast with coffee. She ensured that I ate a healthy breakfast but she herself would gorge on the oiliest and fattiest food possible. She would then gossip around for half an hour with her colleagues and as all of them were that age, their favourite topic used to be marriage. After that gossip session, she used to call me to fill me in with what all who all had bought and what all we needed to shop over the week. She would then go and actually work for some time and have more gossip sessions etc.

I would generally lose interest in what she was saying after around 15 minutes, and she did not even expect me to respond. There were no questions in between, all I had to do was show some surprise at times, pity at other times, and happiness at some other. I used to do this while watching reruns of 'Friends' and after around 45 minutes (it had started with 5 minutes) she would call it a day and

goto sleep. She needed atleast 8 hours of sleep to keep her skin glowing. I really did not mind that. I needed atleast eight hours of sleep to keep my head going.

So this was what life had become now. Monotonous, dull, a little boring, with Kriti providing a brief spark at times, and adding to the monotony at others. It was not that I was being singled out for such a life. All people my age, who were married or were about to be married, or were even thinking of marriage, were in a similar situation. Love marriage or arranged, it really did not matter. Slowly other people around you started vanishing and your spouse became your only companion. I did not know whether it was good or bad but this is what was happening and I was not doing anything to stop it, not that I wanted to. Not that I could.

The marriage functions were to start in the next few weeks. The engagement was the first to come and as the day came nearer, the excitement in Kriti was palpable. There was no such feeling from my side, but I guess she made up for both of us. We were to be engaged in a banquet hall of a decent hotel in Delhi and around a week before the actual date, my parents came to Delhi for all the arrangements. I also took a week off from work. In that way work was good, there was no issue around holidays. Kriti took two off. She would take around a month off for our wedding and the honeymoon which she had been planning since the time we had started talking. She had apparently picked some country in Europe which I could not even spot on a map. I was okay with it. Not that I had a choice.

At times I wondered that was I even ready to be married, and at times I wondered whether I was even a part of the whole marriage, because honestly it did not seem so- I had absolutely no say.

I asked Hari the same question over drinks one day, when we were both pretty high. He looked me straight in the eye and said "Even I am not yet ready for marriage. And I even have a kid. I don't think even he is ready for marriage. I mean, I don't think I would be ready for marriage even when he gets married. You get what I mean right? Men......"

He then stood up to address everyone in the bar, not that anyone was listening, not that anyone really cared about two middle aged drinking men.

"Men are never ready to be married. That is the way we have been made. We are only ready to drink." He said this and finished his drink in one go. Or atleast he tried to finish it in one go.

He took a couple of sips and then quietly sat down and said in my ear. "I had promised my wife I will not be drunk and come home. She says it leaves a bad impression on the kid. I said that the kid cannot differentiate between the toilet and my lap yet. He really would not mind a drunk daddy. And then, she said that it leaves a bad impression on the kid. But this time" he made a hand gesture and spread out his arms as wide as he could. "This time, she said it in a loud voice."

His voice tone also became loud while he was saying this. And then he spoke like a little mouse in a loud whispering tone "And I had to listen. But you bloody dog made me drink so much. I am going to complain about you to her."

He said this, and did finish the rest of the contents in one long swish. I missed the old Hari. The Hari who would puke every time he would get drunk. I missed the old Hari, not the puking, but I looked at him and could see myself very well playing the same part. I guess we were not 25 anymore. We had to grow up. He had grown, it was now my turn. And I guess I was ready to be married. I could lead my life the way my wife wanted. What the hell, I was already doing that with the gym and the weekend shopping and the Italian food and Subway dinners. Plus, when I was married I would get to sleep with her as well. Didn't sound that bad. In fact, it was better than what was happening right now.

Just then Hari got up and rushed to the toilet to puke. He had not changed, he was still the same old Hari. He had managed well and so would I.

Hari came back. He had done what he gone to do and had splashed water all over his face to look a little alive. "Do I look drunk?" He was supposed to ask me this question but he went to the next table and asked.

There was a couple sitting there. "Wait, when I had gone to the loo, you were sitting alone. And now, you are with a girl. And wait, this girl" he pointed at the girl not with his finger but with his whole hand "This girl does not look like Kriti. Not bad man, you found another girl. Good for you. Don't worry, I will not tell Kriti."

He was laughing and patting the back of the guy who was sitting on the other table. The guy on the table was perplexed. But more was the girl sitting with him. She shouted at the guy "Who the hell is Kriti." Hari spoke up. "Didn't he tell you. They are getting engaged next week and married in four months. The whole world knows about it. Kriti has made sure everyone knows about it. How come don't you know?"

He signalled to the waiter and asked "You know right this guy is getting married to Kriti?" The guy didn't know what to say. The girl started blabbering and shouting and cursing when I had to intervene. "Sorry sir, ma'am. This is my friend and I apologise for what he has done. Actually, we are sitting on the table next to you and he is a little high so sir, he mistook you to be me and I am getting married to Kriti so ma'am there is no need to worry for you."

I said that and we left it to the couple to sort out their discussion. Hari sat in front of me and gave a smile. I spoke. "You bastard. You knew it was someone else. You played them on just like we used to."

"Yes you bloody asshead. But unlike earlier times, where you used to join me in the fun and put the poor guy in more trouble, this time you actually saved him."

"I thought you really made a mistake this time. You are really drunk."

"Dude, what do you think? I want my son to see a drunk daddy when I get home? I am a little drunk but I now know how to control myself so that I can behave myself in front of the little dude. I love him man. And I tell you a little secret." Hari came really close to me "I love him more than I love you."

That last secret really meant something. The two of us had been inseparable since the time college had started and what we shared was much much more than mere friendship. I looked at Hari and noticed a change. A change for the better. I knew he was drunk and would never be able to get sober before he got home, but I knew he really wanted to.

And that mattered.

And then I was really ready. I was ready to take the path Hari had taken and had walked on pretty well so far.

The next few weeks passed in a breeze and the day was finally here. It was the day I was to be engaged. An engagement is usually not that big a function with only close friends and families invited. My engagement was no different. I was wearing a formal three piece suit and my bride to be was wearing a red lehenga. Red really did go well with her, it goes well with fair skin and she was as fair as they get. She was looking out of the world beautiful.

All my uncles and aunties from my town and some of my friends from college and work were there and it felt pretty good standing on an elevated stage with a beautiful woman next to me. It was a sense of achievement of sorts. Some of them might have a better job than me, might be earning more than me, but I had the prettiest wife! I think Hari understood the look which I was giving. His wife was also very pretty and he would have felt the same I guess.

He came upto me, gave me a hug and said in a my ear. "Don't worry dude, after a few days, even Madhuri Dixit becomes boring."

He had a mischievous twinkle in his eye and we both burst out laughing. He somehow looked as if he had had alcohol but there were no traces of that anywhere near. He stood around while Kriti introduced me to her extended family. He offered me his glass of Coke. I said no. After two minutes he again offered it to me and whispered in my ear "After a few sips, even Coke tastes like vodka."

He winked at me. "And after a few sips of vodka, even aunties look like angels."

I quickly took the glass from him and gulped it down in one go. I think it had more alcohol in it than the Coke but it made me feel good. All of a sudden, I had a bigger smile on my face. I really did feel happy.

The time came and we exchanged rings. She had selected a pretty expensive one for herself. It had made my wallet lighter by around Rs. 1.5 lakhs. She said that with the ever rising prices of metal and rock, this was to be thought of as an investment rather than a gift. If I had used that amount of investment on my car, I would be driving around with a much bigger boot but that was besides the point. Plus, the ring which her parents had selected for me was not bad either. It had cost them around 2 lakh rupees but in India if you are father to a girl, get ready to spend ridiculous amount of money for your son in law.

The ring exchanging part took us a long time. She wanted it to be done in a typical English wedding style, minus the kissing the bride part of course. Hari posed as my best man, a drunk best man who had tried, and in fact mildly succeeded in making the groom drunk, and she surprisingly had her room mate, about whom she could not stop complaining day in day out, as her bridesmaid. I could not understand it. Maybe it was to make her feel jealous that Kriti was now getting married and her roommate was still single. I really could not understand girls. Plus, it was not that Kriti was getting engaged to her beloved Shah Rukh Khan, she was getting engaged to me! Why the jealousy?

So the rituals of our engagement were played out in the form of a traditional English marriage. There was no priest but there was a pandit who was overlooking the proceedings and not looking very happy about it. Unlike the usual marriages, where he used to speak Sanskrit shlokas which no one understood, here he was to read lines written by Kriti herself.

He started with the lines and asked Hari to come forward and hand me the ring. Hari was lost gazing at something on the ceiling. I think he had a little too much of the Coke. A little push from my mother helped and he came forward, there was music and he did an impromptu jig, went down on one knee and handed me the ring. I had been scared all this while that he was handling such an expensive thing but finally I had it in my hands. I saw his wife with their kid staring at him. I knew he would get all this back when he reached home. A big smile appeared on my face. Maybe I too had too much of the Coke.

Next it was Nidhi, Kriti's roommate's turn to hand her the ring. There was again the music but there was no jig from Nidhi. She just walked up, gave the ring to Kriti and went back, without even a hint of a thing called a smile or emotion. But here reaction led to a big smile on Kriti's face. She had succeeded in mission 'jealousy.' Girls.

Kriti really wanted to take the traditional Christian route so now it was the time for the wedding vows. Hari had helped me prepare mine, in fact, he had prepared mine, so I did not expect any miracles. It was decided that Kriti would read them first and I would follow. But she apparently got stage fright and nudged me to go first. And then I got stage fright.

All of a sudden, all eyes were on me. All this while, all the eyes had been on Kriti as she was the one who was looking so breathtakingly beautiful and I was the lucky one who just happened to be there to complete the couple. But now, everyone was staring at me. And I had to speak.

I had memorised the lines a million times. I wanted to surprise Kriti with the vows. I knew I could not really write anything worthwhile, so I had thought that I might as well memorise the lines instead of reading them from a sheet of paper. But I was standing on the stage shell shocked for a complete ten seconds with every eye on me. Even the panditji, who was looking haggard so far, looked at me with expecting eyes.

Then I looked at Hari. He was for some reason pointing at his chest. I then remembered that as an afterthought, he had out the piece of paper along with my handkerchief in the breast pocket of my three piece. He really was the 'best' man. He had saved the day. I then confidently took out the sheet of paper. I opened it and tore it into pieces and I started.

"You know what Kriti, I had written a lot of romantic things on this piece of paper. But honesty, all those were just words, words which made me look good and made you look pretty. They were words which would lead to some 'awws' and 'ohhs' from the girls here in the crowd, but they are more a result of google search on wedding wows by me and my great friend Hari rather than what I really think about you."

Hari waved to the crowd as if he had completed a test century and got another look from his wife.

"So let me start with the real reasons on why I am marrying you. Let me speak straight from the heart, and as you say, I don't really do that very often, so let me try here. First of all, Kriti, I have known you for more than four months now and honestly speaking, I was a little unsure of marriage when we met. It was not about you, it was this feeling that every guy gets before he settles into a life of lifelong commitment. But with each passing day, as I got to know you, I realised that this was the reason I was still 30 years old and not married. All my life I had been waiting for you."

I could see a little tear in her eye. Whatever I had said was not overly romantic, but I think it was the situation and the very fact that I was speaking which got to her.

"Every little detail about you makes me want to spend the rest of my life with you. Remember the day my car broke down, and you haggled with the auto driver for five rupees. That day I was sure that you could manage, in fact you could make us both manage, even if I stop earning from today itself. The way you made me shape up to fit into the marriage photos, made me sure that you will always take care of my health using one pretext or the other. The way you looked at me when we decided on the wedding rings made me sure that no one else's smile could make me so happy. And the way you look not only now, but every day, further makes me sure what a good wife you will be."

I heard a cheers and a wow from the crowd on the last line.

"Kriti, this is the first time I am actually saying this, and I know it would have been far more romantic and personal if it were just the two of us in this room and not 200."

I heard a "Our eyes are closed. You love birds can do anything you want." This evoked a few laughs in the crowd and even brought a smile to the teary eyes of Kriti.

"Kriti, I love you. Will you give me the honour of waking up with you every morning, will you give me the honour, of making breakfast for you, of having Italian food with you, the honour of being forced to goto the gym because of you, the honour of seeing that smile in your eyes every passing moment, the honour of calling you my wife."

And she broke down. Before anyone else could say anything, Hari came and gave me a big hug. "Marry him Kriti or honestly, I will. Believe me, there were stories in college and not all of them were false."

This evoked some more laughs from the crowd and a teary eyed Kriti just nodded and I put the finger on her ring.

"And not to forget that you are so damn beautiful."

More cheers and it was now her turn. She started to speak, but the tears would just not stop. She tried again, and more tears. I went ahead and took her in my arms and there was applause from the crowd. She then took charge over herself and started.

"I don't know when, how or where it happened. It wasn't love at first, but love, just happened. Maybe it was the day I saw you, or maybe it was the day you started listening to me."

She gave a mischievous smile from behind those tears and I reciprocated with one as well.

"In fact it was the day you started listening to me that I decided that I want to marry you. Hehe. But on a more serious, and true note, I knew it was you after the first time we went out. You treated me not like a girl, but like a lady. Every small little thing you did, and still do, like opening the door for me, wait for me to be seated before you sit, always pass the menu to me first. Above all, it is these little things that a girl looks for in her partner. She looks for respect, and then she looks for love. That is the path you followed.

Even I had so much written in so many sheets of paper for this very moment, but as you said, I will also speak straight from the heart. The day your car broke down and I haggled with the auto driver, I noticed that you spent almost the whole night at the mechanic to ensure that such a thing never happens again, the day you started sweating it out in the gym to get into shape for today's pic, I knew that you will do anything to make me happy, the way you looked at me when I finally selected the wedding ring after days and days of shopping made me sure that no matter what, you will always hang in there for me. And the way you look at me not only now, but every day, further makes me sure what a great husband you will be. I have said this many times before, but mainly in front of the mirror and never in front of you. And I really don't care if there are 200 people in this room or just the two of us because no moment could be more romantic. I love you."

There was a huge applause from everyone present and she placed the ring on my finger.

That was it, we were officially engaged now. Just then all the lights went out. I heard Hari's voice over the microphone. "Ladies and gentlemen, as a tribute to the very dashing to be groom and way out of his league beautiful to be bride, we have prepared a little something for them."

A screen appeared out of nowhere and music started playing and photographs from my childhood started appearing. It was a collage of all my greatest memories- graduation pics, pics when I got my first job, my first paycheque, my first gift to my mother with my first paycheque, admission to the business school, graduation from b school, the day I met Kriti for the first time etc. Then there was a similar collage of her photographs with similar details.

It was beautiful, and just like that, the evening was over. I was engaged. As the engagement was more of a family affair with no alcohol, atleast no alcohol officially, I had to take my friends out for a drink to celebrate the end of my freedom. It was an only guys night out and Kriti jokingly asked me to stay away from Hari and left to be with her parents. There were 8 of us guys and we went to a new bar which had just opened in Gurgaon. It supposedly had great live music and a great blend of cocktails. We settled into the bar and ordered a round of drinks. All lights then went out and all the focus shifted to the stage. Apparently some locally famous singer from US was playing. She had recently started making a mark on the American stage. The lights went out, and then all of them shone at one bright spot on the stage.

She was in a black dress. She was fair, had a dimpled chin which gave a something special to her smile, long eyelashes, curly at the end, like a princess would want them, kajal around her eyes, kajal to keep away the bad omen from her beautiful face, a small parrot nose, which twitched when she frowned, and black flowing hair, which I would later know, she thought were brown.

It was Shalini.

1992

The first time I met Shalini was in the early nineties when twelve year old boys still had innocence and girls still had the elusive charm.

After a whole torturous year, class seven was finally over. Kids say that they gradually start liking school as they grow old, but that is not true. They actually start liking the girls they goto school with. And as girls grow from class 5 to class 10, they obviously look better. School just happens to be there. School is like the necessary evil, like milk in chocolate milk.

But my life had always been screwed up. So I had gone to an all boys school in a small but pretty little town up north. The only thing that grew in that school was my, and other boy's, moustache and beard. And we did not shave, so it hung around, just beneath our faces, like the nest of a very little bird.

So basically, I hated school. I hated getting up, I hated getting ready, I hated taking out my bike, even though I used to like riding it at other times, I used to hate getting late, I used to hate the punishment on getting late, I used to hate the morning assembly, I used to hate the bullies, I used to hate the nerds.

So I guess you get it that I basically hated everything about school. But now it was over, over for a month atleast. I had passed class seven, had done decently if not too well in the exams that happen after every class. My parents were happy, I had actually outdone my best performance with respect to rank in the class, and I was happy, as my parents were happy which meant I would now sleep till late, ride my bike with the destination not being the school gates, play out in the field for much longer durations, not fake studying when at home, read books (comics) out of will rather than force.

Nothing could beat the holidays that come after exams are over. You still do not have the new class books, so your parents really can't make you study, and school starts after around a month. Life gets into good shape. It was during the long break after class seven that my parents decided to take me out on a holiday. In fact a holiday had been used as a bait for me over the last two months to get me to study. We were not very rich people. As was the custom in the days when they got married, my mother was a house wife while my father ran a provision store. The store did well enough to feed the three of us, and the earning had to be stretched to ensure that I went to a good school, but it never made enough to allow the little luxuries like holidays. My mother was looking forward to the holiday much more than I was. She was so happy when I got a good result. The entire year she had spent threatening me, loving me, and using all other methods which only a mother can, to make me study had borne fruit, and she was going on a holiday. Life was good. In fact, the last holiday I remember we had was when I was in class 2, so it really had been a long time.

This was a time of celebration. I had achieved what my parents had hoped for, I had got good marks and a decent rank in the class and the dreams of middle class Indian parents are restricted to only that, that their children study and lead an honest life and have the same dreams for their children. That was the reason for the expensive school. My parents wanted to give their best shot at my education, and hoped, that I would too. And looking at the results, I had not disappointed them.

Even though school was over and the next class had not yet started, my father would not let me sit at his provision store. He always thought that I was meant for something bigger. So my mother and I would sit at home the whole day and would discuss where we would go and what all we would do. The very mention of a holiday had brought a bigger smile to the ever jovial face of my mother and I shared her excitement. We both, after days of deliberation had finally decided Bombay as our destination.

Both of us loved hindi movies, even though we did not get to watch too many, and Bombay was our Mecca. But then, one day something happened that changed the plan. Dad came home late one day and told us that one of his creditors had run away from town. He did not owe dad too much money, but I looked at my mom and I could see the stars in them dimming. She looked at me and regained composure the way only a mother can. She told my father that we could forgo the holiday. And she said it with so much conviction and without a hint of remorse, just like a wife can, to make her husband feel better. The holiday was what she had looked forward to for the last couple of months, or maybe even years, and she was being denied that. My dad looked down. He was a good man who had always wanted to keep his family happy. And he had succeeded so far in life and there was no way he was going to let us down this time. He told us that he would lend some money and would take us out. Not as far as we had wanted to go, but to New Delhi, the capital of our country.

My dad went to the railway reservation counter the very next day so that no other creditor could have a say in our holiday. We were to leave in four days and never had I seen my mother so excited. In fact, never had I seen myself so excited. After 4 long days and even longer nights, the day was finally here. I packed all my good clothes, a pair of jeans, a cap, sunglasses, some t shirts and I was ready. Then my mother packed in some more of my stuff and I was really ready. My mother also packed all her good clothes and she was also ready. My dad packed a smile, and that was what that holiday meant to him, satisfaction for his family.

We lived in a small town and the railway station was no more than 20 minutes from our place, but we still reached 2 hours before the scheduled departure. My mother and I were all dressed up, I had a cap on and sun glasses which were too big for my face. I thought I looked like the most handsome guy in the world and if no one else, atleast my mother would agree to that. In full excitement we got off the rickshaw that had been carrying us only to learn that the train was 3 hours late. We could have easily gone back home and could have come back well within time but my dad decided that the holiday had begun, so we stuck around.

Luckily, it wasn't too hot that day and I went around, exploring the place. I think I used to act a little too young for my age, or maybe it was the nineties, but I still got my kicks by climbing up and running down stairs and running after dogs or cows or whatever animals. My parents had found a bench and were sitting there while I was upto my usual banter. I wandered off and returned 10 minutes later to my parents, cap in hand and sunglasses in pocket. My parents had apparently made some friends and I was introduced to them.

Dad: "Beta, say hi to Sharma uncle. Like us, he is also going to Delhi on a holiday."

I scowled. I did not want a new uncle to tag around in my holiday which I had achieved. But I was a nice boy, so I folded my hands and said Namaste.

Sharma uncle: "Beta, which class are you in. Class 5?"

Okay, I did look young for my age. But class five? I mean, come on. I looked at my mother. I know she knew what I wanted to say-"Why don't you let me shave so that I can look atleast my age if not older?"

To be honest to her, I hardly had any facial hair. She understood and tried to save the day.

Mom: "No bhaisaab, he has just passed class seven. And he has done very well in his exams."

She added the last part to make me happy. But the damage had been done. I looked as if I was in class five. I saw a dog and was about to leave the scene of embarrassment and play with the dog when

Uncle's Aunty came from the restroom, a big bag on one side and Shalini on the other.

That was the first time I saw her. That was the first time she saw me.

She was in a pink dress. She was fair, had a dimpled chin which gave a something special to her smile, long eyelashes, curly at the end, like a princess would want them, kajal around her eyes, kajal to keep away the bad omen from her beautiful face, a small parrot nose, which twitched when she frowned, and black flowing hair, which I would later know, she thought were brown.

And I was sweaty from playing with the stairs, smelly by running after, and finally catching the animals, had my cap in my hand and my sunglasses in my pocket. I pulled out my glasses and wore my cap. I had to make a good first impression and I somehow hoped the oversized cap and glasses would help.

They really didn't.

I was introduced to aunty and Shalini was introduced to my parents. We were not introduced to each other though. As it turned out, Shalini Sharma studied at an all girls school. She lived in a town a couple of hundred kms from our place and was changing trains to goto Delhi for their holiday. She was a year younger to me and was in class six (her father thought I was in class five but that is besides the point). I had never seen her before in my life but I was sure that

I would really want to see her many more times. The two families sat at the bench and the elders started talking. Her father also had some small business and her mother was also a house wife. So they had their common interests. I on the other hand had never interacted with a girl in my life and the girl I wanted to interact with at that point in time did not seem very interested.

I kept the glasses on. They helped me stare at her without being caught. There was a certain uneasiness in the Sharma family but I did not pay much head to it. Time flew by, I did not care about the puppies, and cows and cats around me, all I did was stare. And then the train came and we got onto our different coaches.

The train journey was going to be a long one as our train had already been late and was now being pushed even further. We were going to be in the train for the whole night. It was just a five hour journey but had been extended.

The journey started, with Shalini in some other coach and me practically forgetting about my trip. I sat there, idle, nothing to do and gradually dosed off. When I woke up, around a couple of hours later, the train was still, and sitting with us was the Sharma family. The two families had taken an instant liking to each other. Sharma uncle noticed that my eyes had opened and said

"Bete, goto sleep. Young kids need sleep."

He smiled. I hated him more than I hated anything in the world. I got up and put on my cap and glasses, and tried to act grown up. Shalini was sitting right in front of me, looking out of the window, oblivious of my presence. And I was looking at her. Oblivious of anyone else's presence. This continued for around an hour and then the sun went down and it became dark so she stopped looking out of the window. I thought I had a chance to talk to her but she closed her eyes and lay still. I continued what I was doing.

The Sharma family had exchanged their seats on the train and now we were on the same coach. There was a certain uneasiness in the family, especially Sharma aunty, but I could not figure what it was. Plus, there were better things to think about. An hour later, Shalini was woken up and the two families shared the food they had packed.

So far we had not said a word to each other. We finished the aaloo poori in about half an hour and it was time to goto sleep. I wanted to goto the top berth and sleep but Mr. Sharma again said that little kids should not sleep on the top as they might fall. My mother tried to defend me by saying that I was not a little kid but a 'big boy'. A big boy who had to be saved by his mother. And all this happened right in front of Shalini.

Damn.

I was not in a mood to fight. So I quietly slept on the bottom turf, dad on the top turf and mom in the middle one. The same was repeated in their family. The lights were switched off. I removed my cap and kept it right next to me, just besides my sunglasses, just in case I woke up at night and saw Shalini. I dozed off.

I think I had been sleeping for 3 hours, though you can never be sure of such things, when a gentle hand covered my mouth. My eyes opened, terrified of what was happening when I saw Shalini in front of me. Her one finger on her lips, and the other one on my mouth. She removed the one from my mouth and held my hand and pulled me out of my berth. And she spoke, "Let's go."

I took my cap and glasses with me. And we moved out of our little cabin and went near the open door of the train. The train was moving at a speed I had only imagined to ride my bike at, the door was open and the night was beautifully lit by a half moon. She went and sat at the open door, her legs hanging outside. Her hair flowing all over. I was a brave heart myself. I mean, I used to pick up rats, lizards, insects and all other gross things. But never would I be sitting at the gate of a train moving at a speed of more than 70 kmph with my legs out. Haha, I was a daredevil, not a fool.

Just then she looked back and said spoke again: "Sit here?"

She had such a serene look around her. I could not say no. I had to prove to someone in the Sharma family that I was not a boy but was a man. I tiptoed and sat next to her. First thing, my cap flew off. I stretched my hand but I was never going to catch it. She giggled. I smiled the 'embarrassed smile'. She looked into my eyes and spoke. "You look better without it. And please do not take out those sunglasses now. I know you were staring at me the whole day. They are not as dark as you think they are."

She smiled and then looked away. Her hair were now on her face and she moved them and put them behind her ear but they struggled their way back and she repeated the process. It was beautiful. She had a serene smile on her face. A smile which showed achievement, a smile which showed confidence. The train passed over a bridge and we could see the water beneath our feet and the moon shining in it. We sat like that for I don't know how many minutes.

She pointed towards the sky and spoke: "Don't you wish you were like an aeroplane? Free to wander about anywhere you want."

Me: "I don't know. I am kind of scared of heights." I spoke and I knew it was the wrong thing to say.

She looked at me, giggled some more and got up ready to leave. I could not understand what had just happened and followed her back to our respective berths. That was the first time in my life I did not sleep at night. Something had happened. And that something kept me up all night. And no, it was not the fact that I had lost my cap. I had studied in a boy's school my entire life and it being the early nineties, there were no other places where you could meet girls. So my interaction with them was limited to my female cousins, and some family friend's daughters who used to tie me a rakhi every year. So I had never really had a 'girl' friend, or even a female friend. In school, we had heard stories about some of the popular guys going for walks with them but that was also purely hear say. No one I had known personally had ever interacted with a girl in a non sisterly manner. And then, this happened. And that too, to me.

Lots of thoughts crossed my head that day as I lay in my lower berth. I admit that the thoughts started with the lost cap but then they gradually took more substance. I tried to look at Shalini but she had covered her face with a blanket. My eyes strained to have one more look at her, just to see her smile once more, just to hear her talk once more. I looked at the blanket she was in and kept smiling, at myself, at the world for making such a beautiful creation. I don't know what had happened but this was the first time such a thing had happened and it felt different. It felt a good different. The train moved on as I kept staring into the dark and smiling. That journey had been the best ten hours of my life so far. I felt alive, I felt grown up, I felt something which I could not explain.

Time passed by, bringing the memory of her laughter. I had just heard her some 4 hours ago but it already seemed an eternity, and the sunlight started peeping its way into our little compartment. The rays hit the adjacent lower berth and Shalini moaned and removed the blanket from her head. Her hair were still on her face and I don't know how but there was a smile on her face.

I think she had been thinking the whole night as well. She looked at me staring at her and I did not look away. We looked into each other's eyes and then she slowly pulled the blanket back over. Unfortunately, the sun rays also reached the middle and upper berth and within 10 minutes, everybody was up. Delhi was half an hour away. Shalini was still in kind of a slumber and had her head on her mother's shoulder with her mother's dupatta covering her. I sat stoutly on my seat, trying not to look too interested. I put on the sunglasses but remembered that they were not as dark as I thought they were. The train groaned its way into the Delhi railway station and that was the end of the journey. Both the families got off.

We had hotels in different parts of the city and with no mobile phones back then, coordinating sight seeing was going to be difficult. My parents said their good byes to the Sharma family and took their address to write them a letter some time. Both parties knew this was not going to happen but it was a courteous thing to do. Shalini was going away from me and there was nothing I could do about it. I felt so helpless and little. They called a coolie and the coolie lifted their belongings. We did not need one. Both the families went up the stairs and that is where it was to end. Both had to go in different directions. Our parents shook hands, our mothers embraced and I stood there staring at her. She was five feet away and that was probably the last time we were to see each other.

I wanted to go and say the last goodbye and I trusted my eyes to do the talking. I had the sunglasses on but I knew she could see right through them. Just then she moved forward, we were a foot apart. She put forth her hand. We shook and that was the end of it. The rest of the holiday was fun but was incomplete. My mother was really excited during the entire trip and she made us do all the tourist stuff. I actually quite enjoyed it but it would have been better had Shalini been there. We went to Qutub Minar, and even though I was scared of heights, I went all the way upto the eighth floor and I bought some binoculars to find her from there. We went to the red fort and I kept looking back as I thought that I had caught a glimpse of her in the crowd. We went to the Lotus Temple and I prayed to see her again. We went to India Gate and I imagined her eating ice cream with me.

The five days of holiday were finally over and we got back to the train station. We were to now resume our duties of a bread winner, a home maker, and a laborious student. But there was an excitement of meeting her at the railway station again. But such things never happen. We had an uneventful journey back home with no sitting with strangers near the open door at night. Real life was back. We were home

6 YEARS LATER
1998

The next few years of school life after the Delhi holiday were to be very important as I had to decide on a career. Or atleast that is what my parents and elders said. The years came and went without much happening as I used to be surrounded by books for most of the duration. I was a decent student and in class twelve had put in an extra effort and had made it to a grade A engineering college. My parent's wishes were now completely fulfilled and I was allowed a bit more freedom in those days. My interaction with girls was however still limited to that one encounter with Shalini and the more I thought about it, the more I had an urge to go to her town looking for her. But I let the urges be. I tried to convince myself, and partially succeeded, that I meant nothing to her and that she would not even recognise me.

My college was in Delhi and I felt a little alone during the first few months I was in hostel. My mother cried when I boarded the train to Delhi and Dad just looked down. I know he had a tear in his eye but he was a man and could not show it. But I was still a boy. That was the second night in my life I could not sleep at night. I thought about the wonderful years I had as a kid with my parents. The way my father used to tell me a story to make me sleep every night when I was young, and my mother would play cricket with me when my father was away. How both of them had left all worldly pleasures to ensure that I get good education and the look on their face when the results came out and I had finally made it. And how unfair it was of me to leave them like this when they needed me more than I needed them. I knew that things would never be the way they were. All we had to show for the last 17 years- were memories. Very very pleasant memories.

I wiped my tears with my hand and convinced myself that I had played the part of a good son by studying hard and going where I was. But the thoughts just came pouring in and I finally reached Delhi. This was to be home for the next 4 years atleast, if not more. I got off the train and looked around at the milieu of people at the station. All having a place to go, all having work to do, and even in all that crowd, I felt alone. Alone in a new city which I now had to call home.

I hired a coolie and reached the prepaid auto taxi stand and started my first journey to my college. I made small talk with the auto driver and asked him about the city in general. How the people were, how strict were the rules and regulations, and other such questions which face you when you come to live in a big city from a small town. He was a nice guy, and told me about the city. It was good to the rich and bad to the poor. The rich had their air conditioned cards, their big houses, the money to buy pleasure. The poor had the scorching sky as a roof, the police running after them, and the rich ridiculing them. He continued about the misery of the poor, which I guess emanated from his own life. We stopped at a red light and right next to us stopped a scooter. The father was riding with the mother in pillion. A little boy, around five, was standing on the scooter, in front of his father. He looked at me and smiled. A smile not only from the lips, but from the eyes. I smiled back. My auto driver had forgotten to talk about the people in between the rich and the poor. The people like me, and the little boy on the scooter next to me. The middle class. Life was going to be alright. Delhi already felt like home.

The journey continued and I saw the college gates and felt proud of myself. The journey of life was going to begin.

The first few months of college were a time when the freshers kept a low profile. There was the usual ragging in the hostels, but nothing out of the ordinary. I met Hari the second day we were in college and that was a friendship that was to last for a lifetime. He was also from a small town, but from the eastern part of the country.

Girls seemed to be a new species to me and I was overly intrigued by them at first and then in completely awe of them. This was the first time that I was studying in a co ed system of education. My only meaningful interaction with the fairer sex had been in that train journey and I was a little uncomfortable around them. But as we got talking, exchanging notes, and at times, even going for movies with them, I began getting a little more comfortable. I learnt that girls were just like guys. They were insecure, they were alone, and they also wanted good and genuine company.

I had started shaving now and looked the part of a seventeen year old. I had an athletic frame, was decently tall at 5 feet some inches, had the skin color typical of an Indian, wore glasses, not the ones to keep out the sun but the ones which come when you watch too much television or study too much. I had the normal small town boy hair for the first few months which I later started to style in a different manner.

There was a girl name Roshini, who was from Delhi, and we both kind of developed some kind of a bond. It was the first time I had a 'girl'friend and I started to enjoy her company more than the company of guys around me. She had a different perspective of things and I liked her point of view. She was not utterly beautiful, but was pretty in a non conventional way. And when you really start liking someone, looks cease to be important. And I think she started having a thing for me as well. But I used to be a pretty focussed guy at that time. Focussed to make a good career for myself, to earn money so that I could take care of my parents and make them live the life they had dreamt for me. It had taken me a lot of effort to reach the college of my choice and before I had come here my mother had told me, in no uncertain terms, about what affect a girl can have in your life. And I had not been in hostel long enough to disregard what she said. I guess Roshini's mother would have said the same to her as I could see something in her eyes. She wanted to say something, but just could not. I think she would have seen the same in mine.

I guess, at that time, with her, that was enough.

We started hanging out quite a lot during those days. She was a nice girl. Different from other girls, but yet the same. Honest, but yet holding something back, serious, but yet fun.

The days of college kept passing by and were made beautiful by the very presence of Roshini. Slowly the things that my mother had told me before I had left for hostel stopped making sense. Slowly I thought that having a girl to love would only make me more secure, slowly, I started to have the urge to be more than just friends. We used to go on dates, me and Roshini. We never called them dates, but that is what they actually were. If you go out with one girl, for more than 5 times a week, it is a date. But we never called it that. And I think that even she had slowly forgotten what her mother had told her about young boys. Even she was reciprocating.

This went on for around 4 months and we were in December. It was the college fest period and a time where even 'dedicated to studies' or nerd type of people, like Roshini and I, could take it easy and relax. On one Sunday, when our college fest was on, I had asked Roshini for breakfast and she had agreed. I could not sleep the night before that, the third time in my life such a thing had happened. I knew that something had to be said, something had to be done, but my upbringing could not let me come out with it yet.

I was too scared.

If she said no, I would lose a friend, and if she said yes, I would lose my mother's trust. It was a lose lose situation for me but I knew that it was not possible to continue the way things were. We had decided to go for breakfast to Connaught Place. I woke up from whatever sleep I had managed and looked at my roommate Hari. He was still in a slumber and I smiled at the easy life he led. He had nothing to do with girls, or books, or with anything for that matter. How he made it to college was beyond me. His only love was cricket. Something he had given up in class ten to study for entrance exams but had pursued with a renewed vigor now that he was in college. As it was winter, the fog would not let him practice for atleast three more hours.

I got out of the bed and went into the balcony. The low lying clouds spread over the cricket field, and the sun just making its presence felt over the horizon gave the morning a surreal look. Some over enthusiastic seniors had taken to jogging and there were some students from other colleges who had come for the fest who were just sitting on the ground, enjoying the warmth of the early rays of the sun. Delhi mornings were beautiful and having breakfast with Roshini was the perfect way to start the day. I got ready quickly, the cold water in the hostel ensuring that my bathing time was limited. I wore a new pair of pants and a new shirt which my mother had sent with a relative who had happened to visit Delhi. It gave me quite the look. Then I removed the shirt and changed into an old one. And then I again changed into the new one. Hari in the meantime had got up and was looking at me and was laughing.

He spoke- "You love her don't you?"

This was the first time someone had actually said it. So far it had been an unsaid thing between me and her, but this was the first time someone had put it down in words. I looked at Hari, smiled, or maybe blushed, and moved out of the room.

Roshini was to meet me at the campus gate. She used to live at home but due to the fest had put up with one of her hostel friends. We were to meet at 7:30 and I got there 10 minutes early. I was waiting at the gate, looking out for her in between the clouds when she appeared. Like a goddess. She was wearing a white salwaar kameez which was camouflaged by the white fog, her hair were open and were wet, first time I had seen them that way. She was around 25 metres from me and it appeared as if she was floating in the air, like an angel, like a goddess. She was looking too pretty. She approached me and for the first time, there was awkwardness between us. We did not know whether to shake hands, give a little hug, or just say a normal 'hi '.

We went with the 'hi.'

Not many words were exchanged as we left the campus gates and towards the road. I was a big believer in letting the eyes do the talking, maybe because I did not have the courage to speak. We stopped an autorickshaw and got in.

The ride to CP from our hostel was a good 20 minutes. The cloth on the side of the auto was down on account of the chilling cold and it was as foggy as I had ever seen. When the ride started, we were sitting on opposite sides of the auto. An unknown easiness had creeped in between us over the past couple of weeks, and had culminated in the morning, but it was not an uncomfortable uneasiness. It was a beautiful uneasiness. We both knew there was something unsaid which our eyes were communicating but our lips had not gathered courage to say yet. And I knew that today, only eyes would not do the trick. I moved a little towards her. She looked at me surprised. Then looked down and then looked up again. The surprise then gave way to a smile and I came even more close. I lifted my hand and put it behind her, on the seat. She moved back and her back touched my hand.

She smiled and said: "It's really cold."

The message had been given. I was just about to put my hand around her when I heard a loud bang. We were stopped at a red light and right next to us, sitting on a rickshaw, a girl had thrown a plastic bottle of water on the windshield of a car.

The moment was lost. I got out of the auto to see what had happened. All I could see was that a girl was running after a car, the occupants of which I assume had tried to tease the girl and had got a bottle of water on their windshield as a prize. The car zoomed away and the girl, in full public, mouthed obscenities which I find difficult to even reiterate. The girl had her hand in the air as if she was ready to slap them but they had now run away. She then turned around and got on the rickshaw. The poor rickshaw guy did not know what had happened to him and was too stunned to move and as a result even he got a mouthful. He started moving ahead.

I was smiling at the whole episode when all of a sudden the girl turned around to see the reaction of the public.

She was in a pink dress. She was fair, had a dimpled chin which gave a something special to her smile, long eyelashes, curly at the end, like a princess would want them, kajal around her eyes, kajal to keep away the bad omen from her beautiful face, a small parrot nose, which twitched when she frowned, and black flowing hair, which I would later know, she thought were brown.

It was Shalini.

The rest of the morning just passed. I was with Roshini, a girl who I had feelings for and who also felt the same for me, in the romantic winter of Delhi, in Connaught Place for breakfast. The setting was perfect but nothing seemed to matter. I could not get Shalini out of my head. The dimpled chin, the flowing tresses, she brought back memories from an era which had been locked in one corner of my heart but was suddenly opened. The way we had first met, the way she had taken me to the train door, the way we had our first conversation. My mind was too preoccupied and Roshini was a little confused as to what had happened. She had expected something to happen between me and her that morning, she had expected me to tell her that I loved her and wanted her to be more than just a friend. But I was completely lost in some other thoughts.

We had our breakfast of sandwiches and coffee and were back in the campus within an hour. Not many words were exchanged in the whole period. Just silence, and not the good silence. This was the awkward silence.

Hari was getting ready when I entered and he saw me and said "You are in love." I just smiled, fell on my bed, and went to sleep. I had things to dream about. I got up around noon and lazed around till the evening. My college had a cricket match in the evening and Hari was playing, so I decided to see that. I knew Roshini might be there and I was wondering as to what I would say to her. But I let it be. I had to support my friend in the match. He was the only first year guy in the team.

The match was a day night affair. We had installed flood lights in the ground and the match started around 4 pm so that it could be over before the fog set in. We were facing some other college from Delhi. I was least interested in cricket but the atmosphere was electric. Our team won the toss and had elected to bat. My usual friends used to be Hari and Roshini. Hari was playing, so he was not there, and there was this awkwardness with Roshini after the morning so we just said 'hi' to each other and she left to be with her other friends. I was sitting alone, in one corner, when someone came and sat right next to me.

"So you liked Delhi that much that you decided to settle here. Not bad."

I was looking down but I knew who it was. A smile appeared on my face.

I spoke "I guess I can say the same to you!"

I looked up, and there she was, right next to me, and talking to me. Shalini.

It felt as if everything stopped for a moment. The noises around us, the lights, the chit chat of the people, the abuses on the field. It seemed as if it was just me, and just her, just like the way we had first talked, just like I had always imagined, just like how I wanted it to be.

She spoke first "Let's go."

I had a moral obligation towards my friend Hari. I had to support him by my presence but just then I saw him walking back towards our team. I looked at the wicket, it was uprooted and the rival team was celebrating. Our man had fallen first ball. "Let's go" I said.

We both got away from the madness of the game to the quite road which enveloped the campus and started walking.

"So, Mr. High Flying engineer is it? Nice college, secure future. Liking it?"

"It's ok. In fact, it's pretty nice. More than I could have asked for. Honestly, more than what I deserved. I have always been lucky with exams. My preparation was never that great that I could make it to such a college. I just had a very good day."

"So what are you studying here? Okay, don't answer that. I am an arts student and I like to maintain my distance from the sciences. Plus I know you nerdy type of guys, once you start, you just don't stop. Leave what you are doing, tell me, it must be fun studying about what you have always wanted all these years."

"Fun? How can studying be fun? I am not doing this to have fun. I am doing this for the things you said before. For a secure future. I didn't like studying when in school and believe me I hate it as much right now. What I am doing is of no interest to me. What comes after this is what I really want. The secure future, the long car, the big house. You know. The happiness."

She gave me such a puzzled and confused look. "So you are telling me, that you do not enjoy what you are doing? That every day, you do not wake up with the feeling that today, I am going to learn something new about what I love."

"No, I wake up groggy and sad that I have to goto college and study physics and maths. I am not a big morning person, plus the whole routine of classes till 5 pm really gets to you. So there is nothing really to look forward to. In fact there is- the holidays."

She again gave me a confused look, but she let it pass. "So, had it not been for a secure future, what would you have liked to do?"

I looked at her. And then I thought. And then I spoke "You know, maybe it is easy for you to say that I am not following my dream but am in this race against myself. That I have given up a good portion of my life trying to do something I do not like. But you know what, maybe all people are not meant to have dreams. Maybe, there are supposed to be people like me. Because honestly, had I not studied hard and had I not been in this college, I probably would not be doing anything. I don't have any grandiose dreams of being a cricketer or being a movie star or making my own music. I am happy in going to engineering college for four years, maybe do a post grad after that, and then work five-six days a week and lead a happy content life. Maybe, that is my dream. Maybe it is not. Maybe I have a dream later in life, but right now, I am pretty content with whatever is happening."

She looked at me and smiled. "Okay. My idea was not to be preachy. It was just that, I cannot imagine just doing something for the sake of it. For example, my board exams are in a couple of months, and here I am, in an unknown city, on an unknown road, running after what I really want."

I was pleased to hear that she did not say 'an unknown person'. A sense of pride filled me

"You really want me? Am I the reason you are here?"

She looked and me and laughed. A giggle which filled her face and made her look prettier than what I could imagine anyone could look.

"Let me reiterate- here I am, in an unknown city, on an unknown road, *with an unknown person* running after what I really want." She smiled, paused and continued. "No you idiot. I was here for the music competition. I cleared the prelims and the final is tomorrow. Idiot."

I gave her a goofy smile. She continued. "My parents asked me not to go. That I should study to get into a good college etc etc. You know how parents are. But what is the point. I don't want to be going to a college and study maths and physics and complain about it." She looked at me, smiled again, and slipped in a sorry. I smiled and let it pass. "I want to sing. I want to sing in front of the whole world and this stage is just the beginning. You wait and see where I reach."

She had this thing in her eyes which made me believe what she said, and I believe eyes more than words. We walked for some more time. She thinking about where her voice would lead her, and me thinking about her.

She spoke again. "So any regrets in life?"

"You know we are too young to be discussing such things. I am eighteen. I haven't lived enough to have major regrets. Though there is one complain I have from God though."

"What is it?"

"That it wasn't a full moon the day we met."

She blushed and said "I have one regret too. And believe me, I think of it every night before I sleep. Why didn't I push you out from the train that day? I could see it on your face that you were shit scared. God! Where do you get such cheesy lines? I am telling you, leave this engineering crap, you should be making a cheesy love story. And as a favour, I will sing in your movie for free."

We both smiled and continued our walk and reached the place where the girls from outside campus were staying.

"So this is where you have put up right. Your in time is 8:30 and we have only 5 minutes left. I guess I will see you tomorrow then."

She looked at me with those confused eyes again. "I am not going in at 8 30. I am a girl living in a small town. It is not every day that I come to Delhi alone. I am going out to explore the city. If you want to tag along, be my guest, otherwise, yes, see you tomorrow."

She said this and walked right past me, I ran behind her initially trying to convince her to stay back but I knew better. We both marched out of campus and got to the bus stand. We took the next bus which came, not knowing where it was going, not knowing where we wanted to go, but going nevertheless.

The bus was pretty crowded, considering the time, and we were standing very close to each other. My hand was covering her back to protect her. I could sense the uneasiness within me. I wanted to hold her, feel her breath, smell her hair, get closer. We were looking into each other's eyes, me completely lost within, when suddenly, Shalini started moaning.

"Aahh, uggghhh" and then a louder "aaaghhh".

All eyes first went on her, then on me, then on her again, and then on me again.

I gave a "I don't have anything to do with this" look and in a jerk removed my hand from her back but I could see the anger in the people's eyes. Before they could bash me, Shalini spoke

"I am pregnant and I cannot stand. I am in pain." She again made the "aaghh" sound. All the attention suddenly shifted to her. She had no baby bump and even I was confused. Then it all made sense, she had run away from home because she was pregnant and somehow found me and was taking me along to wherever she was going. But this did not make sense even to me. I felt ashamed thinking so.

People started staring at her, looking for an obvious baby bump. But when a girl says she is pregnant, baby bump or no baby bump, you don't ask questions, you have to listen! So a couple sitting right next to where we were standing got up and offered her a seat. She sat down. She let out another "Aaagh" and looked at the lady sitting next to her with a child like face, and then pointed towards me with her eyes.

Clever trick, and I got it a little late. The lady got up and offered me the seat. Apparently I was the father of the imaginary child and I needed to sit with my *wife*.

Believe me, I did not look the part. But then, neither did she. But no one dare question a pregnant woman. I looked at her and I could see the smile within the grimace which she still had to put on as everyone was staring at her.

The rest of the journey was comfortable as we both had a comfortable seat to sit on. When asked by a suspecting aunty, Shalini told her that we were having twins and that she was three months into her pregnancy. She could say all this with such a straight face that it made me laugh in wonder. The bus finally stopped and we got off at the last stop, JNU. From one campus, we rode all the way only to enter another, each with their own ways of life.

We walked around JNU aimlessly, talking about nothing and talking about everything. Shalini told me that she had decided at the age of four that she wanted to do something related to music. She loved the way music could make her sleep, could make her getup, could make her do anything. I said she was lying because at four, some of us are not even toilet trained, but she said all that with such conviction, and with her eyes, that she made me believe every word. There was this passion within her when she talked about music, a passion which was missing in my life so far, and maybe would never come. She made me think for the first time about the choices I had made in life and whether or not they were the right ones. But I let the thought pass. My choices secured me a good salary, her choices, only gave her a dream, which may or may not be fulfilled. I would any day take the long car.

We walked our way around campus and reached the Partha Sarthi rocks, the highest natural point in Delhi and sat down on the top.

If you ever want to take a girl anywhere in Delhi, this is the place. And we happened to chance on it by mistake. The low lying clouds had covered all our surroundings and it seemed as if we were on top of a cliff with eternity beyond us and infinity below. We could hear some rock musicians jamming at some point far away and I could again see the passion within Shalini ignited on listening to the electric guitar. There was an expression her face gave out when she listened to or even talked about music. An expression which told me that her body was with me, but her soul was with the music.

We continued sitting there for four hours. Sitting in complete silence at times, and chit chatting the next. I was as comfortable with her as I would be with anyone in my life. One of my friends had once told me that if you could enjoy silence with a person, when neither of you feel the need to fill in the holes of silence in between the conversations, then, don't let go of that person.

I felt every word of what my friend had said. Shalini asked me what I wanted to do going ahead and I reiterated my plan of a nine to five job with a fat paycheque and this time instead of asking me to follow my passion, she just listened, and listened as if she was really interested. When I finished my story of having two kids, she smiled. I think she really did appreciate what I had thought for myself. I might not have had any passionate dream, but I was focussed, and that is what I think intrigued her. Then she told me what she wanted to do.

Her love for music in her childhood had led her to see music in everything and in every form and learn as many musical instruments as she could. But as she grew, she realised her real calling was singing. She was a trained Indian classical singer and in the last few years had started to dabble into English rock. I told her that I thought that both were very different styles of singing but she went back to the basics that there are only seven notes in music, and your voice had to integrate them together and can do that in any form. She told me she wanted to do shows, she wanted to sing for people, she wanted to sing for herself, that basically, she just wanted to sing. Whatever else happened was just by the way. She looked so lively sitting on that rock with me talking with such an energy about what she loved that time ceased to matter. It flew at one time, and just stayed still the other. Slowly the night got the better of us and we both fell asleep, on top of the rock. I thought I would ask her to sing, for me, but I thought that a better moment for that would come.

I woke up with the first rays of the sun. It seemed as if the trees below us were mountains of snow and the boroughs in between were valleys. The view was a spectacle in itself and next to me was something even prettier. Shalini. Her hair wes covering her face and the gentle breeze was making them sway around. The cold had made her go red on the cheeks. I had given her my jacket at night and she was holding on to it with her tiny pretty hands. I just kept staring at her and then her eyes opened. The most beautiful eyes I had ever seen. I could see the music in them. She saw me and smiled. We both took an eyeful of the scenery in front of us and made our way back to the main road to catch the bus back to my college. It was 7 am.

Her singing competition was to start in 4 hours. Not much was said during the journey back and we parted ways near the girl's hostel. She looked at me and no one said anything. At least, our lips didn't, but my eyes said whatever they had to.

I came back to my room and Hari was already awake. He was ready to go for a jog. He looked at me and repeated the same lines "You are soo in love." I smiled and enacted a duck in front of him. I could not really enact a duck, it was more of a chicken, but he got the point. He had been dismissed on the first ball yesterday, a golden duck. He threw his shoe at me and we both had a good laugh about it. He told me that even though he had failed to contribute; our college had won the match. Apparently the umpire, our sports teacher, had a big role to play in that. We were to have our second match today and Hari was to have his last chance. So he had decided to get up early and go for a jog. I asked him how that would help. He didn't seem to know but he said he was going anyways. The match was scheduled at 11 am. He asked me if I would come and I could not answer.

He understood, put his hand around me and said that I was going to miss a miracle- his batting. I laughed it off and he nodded, smiled and left. I rushed out as soon as Hari left. I had to get something for Shalini. And I knew the perfect gift. I ran till the main gate and took a bus to a place near the main terminal. I got off a couple of stops before and the child was still there. He was selling small flutes. I had noticed them yesterday when I was with Roshini and I just knew how much Shalini would love it. I bought one and came back to the hostel with a big smile plastered on my face. I took a small little nap and then started to get ready. I used Hari's hair gel for the first time. I tried to get a dishevelled look, but then thought that it would appear that I was trying too hard. So I washed it off with water again and got back to my usual style. I wore a black shirt, blue jeans and white sneakers. I was looking charming if not handsome. I shaved for the second time in two days and at 10:30 was ready to go.

I reached the auditorium where the event was happening. The participants had already arrived and I tried to spot Shalini. And there she was, in a blue salwaar kameez, hair neatly tied up, her face devoid of any nervousness but having a confident feel to it. I waved at her and she waved back. The next thirty minutes passed by looking at her.

The focus and importance which she exuded made her look even prettier. And the competition began. All the participants were sitting on the stage. As the prelims were over, there were ten of them and each one of them was given 7 minutes to sing. Shalini was the first to go. She sang a beautiful medley, starting with 'Ae mere watan ke logo..' then changing the mood to naughty with "Piya tuu, ab to aaja.." then going sensuous with "Aap jaisa koi.." and then rounding it all off with Raag Bhairavi. There was thunderous applause when she finished. It was breathtaking. It was beautiful. While singing, I could feel her getting into the song, feeling the emotion, feeling the pain, the joy, the lust, the melody in each of her performances. She was beyond words. Her singing was beyond words. Slowly, the other nine also completed their performance but no one matched Shalini. And then it was time for the results. Our director was the special guest and he came on stage to give away the prizes.

Third prize goes to Raj Malhotra. I was a little relieved. I did not want Shalini to come third. She would be devastated. I looked at her when the prize was announced, she still had the same serene look on her face. Second prize goes to Rajvir Singh. Again a little relief for me, Shalini only deserved the first prize, nothing less than that would do. But now the relief was mixed with a little fear. What if she did not win?

And the first prize goes to Saumya Sharma. That was it, I was heartbroken. I could not lift my eyes up to meet Shalini's, but when I did, not a hint of remorse in them. She still had the same serene look. The director gave a little speech and that time helped me get over the fact that Shalini had not won. As the speech got over and people started to move away, I walked over to her.

"Sorry."

"For what?"

"You were the best but still you did not win, for that."

She smiled. "I came here to sing, not to win. And I did that. I came here for myself, not to get a trophy to be showcased. I am perfectly fine."

She said this with such conviction that either she was a very good liar, or she actually meant it.

"So no regrets?"

"Well, there is one regret."

"What?"

"That I did not throw you out of the train that day." We both smiled and then all of a sudden she said. "It was really nice meeting you but one of my relatives is coming to pick me up and drop me at the station. My train is in 45 minutes. I have to go home."

She said it just like that, with no emotion, with finality. I tried to oppose.

"So when do we meet next?"

She smiled and said "I don't know, but I really hope we do meet."

"You still live in the same town?"

"I do and I would really appreciate if you do not come down to where I live. Middle class parents, you know the rules."

Know the rules, I could write the rule book.

She took my hand and said again "I really do hope we meet again."

"Can I have your number?"

"We don't have a phone."

That was the end of the conversation. I took out the flute and gave it to her. She took it and left, just like that. No looking back to see if I was still standing waiting for her. No tears, no promises, no melody on my gift. Just a hope, that she wanted to meet me again. I followed her for a distance, always trying to hide myself but I knew that she knew I was following her.

One of her uncle's was already at the ladies hostel gate in his car and she got on with her bag. The railway station was a thirty minute ride by car. But I had no vehicle. I ran out to the bus stop and waited for the next bus. The bus would take me 45 minutes to get there.

Nevertheless, I got on, praying to Indian Railways to have a delay on her route. I remembered in which town she lived from last time and when I reached the railway station I heard the announcement that the train to her town was ready to depart from platform 13. I was on platform 1.

I ran. I ran like I had never run before, pushing some passengers and going around the others. By the time I reached, the train had already started moving and slowly, it passed me, coach by coach. I went down on my knees looking at it going past.

I did not see her for 7 years after that.

7 YEARS LATER
2005

It was a lazy Saturday morning. I was on my couch, where I had dozed off after coming back from a party where I had too much to drink and did not remember much after. What the heck, I did not even remember how I got home and on my couch. Wait, was this even my couch?

I somehow managed to raise my head and saw the familiar looking wall with photos of me and my parents on it. Yes, it was my house. I again lay dead on the couch.

It was a regular Saturday morning. Regular for the last 4 years atleast after I had passed out from college. The sun got the better of me around noon time. I had given the curtains for dry cleaning after Hari, in one of his days of stupor, had gone on and on about how he could have been Sachin Tendulkar but how the engineering degree had pulled him down. His frustration, along with all the alcohol he had consumed, along with all the food he had eaten along with a lot of unidentifiable things had come out on the curtain while he was trying to run to the toilet. Well, that is what he said because in reality he was running in the opposite direction of the toilet. Not a pretty sight, I guess you can imagine. In fact it had been a month since I had given them for dry cleaning. I think I should have got them back by now. I made a mental note to check.

I remembered that last night's party had a reason to it. I remembered because I had foot the bill. I tried to remember what it was and slowly got up from the bed to put some water into my system. Yes, vague memories came back. I was being sent to the United States of America by my software company for a six month project. A lifetime dream was finally being fulfilled. Life was good.

I ambled through to the refrigerator and gulped down around half a litre of water. It tasted weird, it was tasteless and not the sweet bitter like beer, but I guess it was ok. Life started to make sense again. The weird twitchy feeling in my throat gave way to hunger. I looked around the fridge, saw some bread, stuffed it in my mouth, stuffed a cheese slice and again got back to the couch which would be my companion for the next hour atleast.

So this is how my life was then. I was 24, going to be 25 in some time. I looked my age, was still five feet something. People say you add a couple of inches during college but honestly you don't. I still had the natural and typical Indian skin color, still the same hair, the style obviously was different- lots of gel, but, I was way cooler than what I was seven years ago. Or this is what I would like to believe. I still had the same friend Hari, but unlike earlier, had some people who bordered on acquaintance and friends. Okay they were my friends but Hari was the only one I was close to. The others were like ok ok friends. People I used to hang out with, watch movies with, get drunk with. Basically chill out with. Life on the whole was pretty different from what it was in college, and was pretty awesome. I had started to live my dream of having decent amount of money in the bank. And girls were no longer something to be afraid of. In fact I had gotten over their fear quite early. I was no longer the small town boy who could not figure out his way in the big city.

I was now a city dude. I know it sounds lame, but that was the way I was back then.

In the first year, I was close to a girl Roshini but completely blew it away when I saw Shalini. After Shalini disappeared from the face of earth, I was a little lost for a few months but then, I was 17, how long can a 17 year old be in love? By the time the first year ended, I had managed to have a steady girlfriend, and had completely ignored what my mother had told me about young girls and young boys.

Surprisingly, her presence had a very soothing affect on me. I started to do better in college, got involved in some extra curriculars, and even stood for vice president when in the third year. I lost the elections but that is a completely different story. The result was much closer than what Hari would tell you.

The years at college past and I got a job within the first week of entering the last year. My grades were good, I was decently presentable, and I got one of the best jobs offered on campus. I think that is what led to my break up. My then girlfriend, Rakhi, had better grades than me and was certainly more presentable than me, but she got a job a notch lower than mine and then there were the fights of me using her for my own good etc etc which got a way bit too much for me and I dumped her. We did not talk for a good 2 years after that but now it was fine.

So yes basically, I had transformed from a small town boy who listened to everything his mother said to a city boy who still cared about his parents, but did so as he pleased. My job placed me in the capital itself and the last four years had been a roller coaster ride. There were the drinks, there were the girls, there were the friends and there was me. Office just happened to be a part of my existence. A big part in fact considering that I used to spend 10 hours a day, five times a week in office. I was working in one of the biggest international software companies and was getting paid decently enough. But it was the weekends I craved for. The two days filled life with hope, with meaning.

Life had been devoid of any steady girlfriend for the good part of the last four years. There were a few brief affairs bit nothing serious. In fact I had recently started flirting with one of my clients from work. Oh shit, I had to meet her for lunch today. Damn. I quickly brushed my teeth and showered. My company had been kind enough to give me a mobile phone and I saw only one missed call on it. That vas a relief. It was already 1 pm. I checked the call, it was from office. I ignored it. Who works on a Saturday? But then like a good employee I called back. It was nothing urgent and could be handled on Monday.

I was always honest to my work, work was what made the weekends possible. I pulled out a blue jeans and a cotton tee and teamed it with semi formal shoes. As an afterthought, I put on a jacket. I looked at myself in the mirror. I looked charming if not handsome. And I had been selected to goto USA for six months atleast.

I quickly applied the daily dose of gel and was ready to go.

I called her, her name was Pooja by the way, and we decided to meet at one of the new coffee shops which had opened in South Delhi. I then had planned to take her to the Partha Sarthi rocks at JNU. That still remained the place where I took girls for a first date and it never failed me. We decided to meet in thirty minutes and I happened to reach there a little early.

I was browsing through the menu and was wondering how many people would want to buy a coffee for 60 bucks in India. This chain had started following the American model of cafes in India but India was so not ready for it. Who would pay that much money for a coffee? I by the way, could afford a coffee so I ordered for an iced coffee and settled down with the newspaper. It was the month of November and the weather had been pretty pleasant when I had left home but now all of a sudden it had started raining. Pooja called me and told me that she would be running a little late as she was stuck in the traffic due to the rain.

Delhi roads, Delhi rains, and Delhi girls.

The more you want to understand them, the more confused you get. I made peace with the fact that she would be a little late and ordered another iced coffee to get rid of the lingering hangover. I browsed through the newspaper and then through the cartoon section. It had been thirty minutes since she had called. I looked out of the glass facade and that is when I fell for her.

This was the first time we were meeting outside office. She worked in a company that had given us a small contract and we had met each other quite often in the office settings. The project was a small one and was nearing its end. It was I who suggested that we meet on a Saturday so that we could close it on time. I basically just wanted to have lunch with her outside the formal confines of an office space and outside the formal confines of a weekday. And there she was. Her hand with a newspaper covering her head from the sudden burst of water, the other hand frantically moving as to make way.

She was wearing a white salwaar with a yellow kurta on top. It was early November and Delhi was just entering the winter stage. She had a shawl wrapped around her in place of the chunni and her short wet hair stuck all around her face as she moved. We had had coffee before, we had had lunch before, in fact we had even had dinner before but it was never the way it was today. Maybe it was because at all earlier points in time we had a laptop in front of us and were discussing how to speed up the project. Or maybe because she was looking so pretty today. She made the final dash to the coffee shop from under a bus stop and had a big smile as she saw me and entered the cafe. She pulled the door but somehow the six inch pencil heels could not support the slippery floor and she slipped and fell with a thud. To add to it, she sneezed. All eyes were on her.

The other young girls giving her a 'why do you wear heels when you can't walk in them' look. The young guys giving her a 'Oh I want to help you but my girlfriend would kill me if I do' look. The older aunties a 'I don't understand why girls are so hooked onto fashion' look. The older uncles a 'what is wrong with the young men of today, had a girl fallen when I was young I would have picked her in my arms' look. And in between all these looks, there was me with a 'I should do something, she is here to meet me and it has not started well' look.

She was pink with embarrassment. It had been ten seconds since she had fallen and so far she had not even tried to getup. She had a scared look on her face analysing the reactions of everyone sitting in the cafe. Everyone was staring at her and she was staring at everyone. The kajal from her eyes had slipped onto her cheeks in the rain and the water had made her eyes go red. Her hair were pressed against her forehead covering parts of her face, her dress was dripping wet when she had entered and falling due to a puddle near the entrance had not helped her cause. I could see water trickling down her cheeks and I was pretty sure it was not the rain. Something had to be done. Someone had to play a hero and who else but me to do it.

It had now been twenty seconds and no one had moved. Time seemed to have gone still. Then, I got up. I walked up to her, gave her my hand and pulled her up. I then lifted her in my arms, my eyes staring down hers, and took her to our table and placed her on the chair amidst a thunderous applause of the people present there.

Well, that is what I should have done. Instead of that, I opened my coffee container and spilled the coffee on the floor of the cafe. Then I sat on the spilled coffee, looked at her, waved my hand and said a sheepish 'Hi.' I don't really know why I did that. Both of us now had a wet ass and I don't think the fact that even I had one made an inch of an difference to her. If anything, I guess she was more embarrassed by my antics that pleased.

No thunderous applause, everyone got back to doing what they were, but I changed the tears into a smile. A goofy smile but nevertheless a smile. She saw me and realised that she did no longer look like the stupidest person in the cafe.

She settled down in the cafe, still wet but atleast not overly concerned about it, and ordered one more of the sixty bucks coffee. She added some chocolate sauce and other things as well making my wallet lighter by 40 bucks more. These cafes were very soon going to go out of business. Who pays 100 hard earned Rupees for a coffee?

We started talking. I made it a point not to talk about what had just happened. The conversation was first the formal self starting about the boring project, but gradually shifted into a friendly banter with office politics and gossips taking centre stage. We went on and on talking endlessly about things which would seem so redundant if I mentioned them now, but seemed so very interesting at that point in time. After around a couple of hours we decided to leave the cafe. Our clothes had sufficiently dried out even though there was a stain on my pants. I put my jacket around my waist to take care of that. The rain had now stopped and the smell of the first rain had enveloped the city leading to a very romantic feel about everything. This time I decided to go with her for a walk rather than the Partha Sarthi rock routine and we strolled in a park close by for 2 hours. She started telling me how much the city had changed over the past few years and the talk, even though boring, seemed interesting to me then. There was something about her which drew me to her. Maybe it was her beauty, maybe something else, but slowly I could realise that I was losing control over myself.

We continued walking around the park. The sun was partly out now and a rainbow was visible if you really strained your eyes. The grass was a very light green with a musky flavour to it. We had removed our shoes and the tiny wet blades ticked our feet as we walked. There were little squirrels running around trying to look for nuts and some leaves had fallen out of the trees due to the rain. The birds, though not singing, but were proudly roaming the sky now that the water had ceased.

I know you can see these things any day of the week. But all this seemed so beautiful and appropriate at that point. I could see myself falling for her. I could see the smile on my face widening with each step we took. I could see myself wanting her more every passing second. And I could see myself loving each moment of it.

Our conversation had now taken a personal tone. The personal tone when you have started working begins with your job and then gradually steers to your life. She pretty much knew about my job so

I just filled in the basic details of how I got there. I started with my modest upbringing, then the college life where I discovered who I really was, and then job where I lived for weekends. And before we could get to her, it started raining again. The small droplets of water started falling on her face. She tried to brush them off initially but then we both made a dash towards the nearest tree. The tree somewhat protected us, but then, we just stopped caring. My eyes met hers and we just stared into each other. I could see that I had had the same affect on her. We got close, then closer.

Then she ran away. Without saying a word, leaving me alone under that tree. I did not know what had hit me. I tried calling her cell phone but she cancelled the call. I tried again and it was switched off. I didn't understand what had just happened. Everything seemed to be going perfectly, but then she just took off. I waited for the rain to subside a little and then made the confused journey back home. I tried calling her for two days but she did not take my call. I would meet her in office on Monday though. My company had to hand over the project to them.

I reached office a little early on Monday. We had an early morning meeting with Pooja's company and irrespective of what had transpired between us, I still had to finish my work. There were some last minute things remaining and the team and I finished them and we were ready. Surprisingly for the other members of my team and expectedly for me, Pooja did not come for the final meeting that day. She had called in sick and one of her colleagues, a more senior guy, had come and understood the processes and the project was over. There would be atleast no more official interaction with Pooja.

I wanted to know what had happened but got immersed in work. November was always a busy period in my company because most of our clients were US based and they never worked in December. So all December deadlines had to be met in November itself. The number of coffee cups on every table increased and the duration of the cigarette and lunch breaks reduced drastically during that period. No matter how laid back at home you may be, when a client needs a project on time, you have to sweat it out at office. I think that is one of the reasons that all major projects, IT atleast , are bagged by Indian companies. Even the people in the west know that if need be we will stay at office all night but will ensure that the work gets done.

It was now 8 pm and I was to have a long day at work. Some of my colleagues had left, while some were still there. I did not have much time so I decided to goto the parantha shop near the base of the building for dinner. My office was on the ninth floor and I took the elevator down. All alone, in a captive little place, you sometimes really do feel if you made the right choices in life. Was this what I really wanted to do? I let the thought pass as it was my job which was going to pay for my paranthas. I walked across the cigarette smoking spot, said hi to a couple of colleagues who were having their last puffs before they headed to a no smoking zone- home. I chatted for a couple of minutes. All of us bitched about how bad things became in November, how it was not our fault that the western world did not work in December and how lousy the salary increments were to be this year and how none of us were going to be promoted and how everyone in the company, barring us, had no work to do and how we had heard that the head of the company was leaving and how someone had seen Shiven and Sonalika in a kind of compromising position and how the quality of the food in the cafeteria had gone even worse and how we should all stop smoking as it is really injurious to health- even the pack said so.

These were the discussions we had every day, and I bet these are the discussions that you can hear around every office every day. These discussions don't really change anything, they just help you vent out the frustration, help you cleanse your system so that you are ready for another session of sitting in front of the computer. I asked the cigarette guy how much I owed him, he said 120 bucks, I said I did not have change and would pay him later. We said our goodbyes and I went out to the local dhaba which served the best aaloo parantha. I usually used to come here with friends and colleagues but today I was alone. It feels weird eating alone in the office. You feel alone, you feel lost, you feel unwanted.

We usually used to order the same paranthas every day but today I had a look at the menu. I was surprised to see the variety on offer. It was not a Punjabi dhaba, apparently they also served Chinese, Mughlai, Continental and Italian. I looked at the menu for a good 2 minutes and saw a spelling error in every dish that was not a parantha. So I ordered two aaloo paranthas with butter and pickle on the side and a two egg double fry with one cup of tea.

Yes, I was not too fat yet, or not too old yet, to think of cholesterol. I liked my food fried. I sat on the garden chair, put my head back and closed my eyes trying to relax and stayed that way for a couple of minutes. When I opened them, expecting to see the waiter with the tea, I saw Pooja, albeit with the tea.

"Hi. Surprised?"

She was still blurry. I needed sleep.

"Well yes, kind off. In fact, yes, very surprised."

She offered me the tea. She had two cups, I took one. She spoke. "I am sorry for what I did. But I had a reason."

"I am sure you had one. Maybe you found me too boring and just wanted to get the hell out."

I tried to be funny and she did smile. Maybe because she had run off earlier and had to do something to make me feel better.

"You know it was not that."

"Then what was it. In fact, never mind. Such things happen. So tell me, how come you are here."

She gave me a look as if I was the dumbest person on earth.

"I am here to see you."

"Really? That's nice." I couldn't think of anything else to say. I really needed sleep. And I needed the aaloo paranthas before the sleep.

She spoke. "Let me put it out straight away. I really. I am. I really am..."

Just then the waiter came with the two paranthas with the butter melting on them and then mixing with the mango pickle. All my attention shifted from her to the food. I was kind of lusting for it.

"Looks nice" she said. "You want some?"

Then I shouted to the waiter "Hero, get one more for madam, aaloo. Then to her "You have to try their aaloo paratha, it is heavenly."

The parantha completely controlled me. She was a little bemused. "I was trying to tell you something."

"Oh yes, please."

"Are you sure you can fathom what I am going to tell you over your loving paranthas."

Her voice had an irritated tone to it. I had dipped a small piece in butter and was mixing it with the pickle but I stopped and unwittingly I kept it down.

"No problem at all. Tell me."

"What I was telling you was that I..."

Just then the waiter came with her parantha. Talk about quick service when you don't need it. She gave the waiter such a dreadful look that he went back mumbling something.

"I really like you."

Wow. I did not know how to react. I knew that she liked me on some level but to actually hear it took me a little back.

"I started liking you soon after we started working together. At first I thought that it was a harmless crush and would pass but as the days kept passing by, it became something more than a crush. And that day, in the park, it got a little too out of control."

I really didn't know what to say, so I spoke "I really don't know what to say."

"But I cannot like you. I mean I should not like you. I am engaged, and that too to my boyfriend of many years. There is a date to the wedding, the cards are printed, invitations are going out. In fact, right now, I should be distributing these cards to some of my relatives."

She took out the marriage invitation from her purse and threw it towards me. It landed close to my food. The cards looked nice, but they would have spoiled my paranthas.

"Then why are you here?"

"I don't know. I don't know."

She started crying a little, then started sobbing.

"I don't know." She sat down next to me. I did not know what to do. I was right in front of my office and a girl was sitting next to me and was crying. And that was not the major problem. She was getting married to her boyfriend, was supposedly out delivering invitations, but here she was sitting next to me and crying.

I really did not know what to do or what to say. "Why don't you eat something. The food is getting cold."

I know, not the right thing to say. She looked at me, gave a disgusted look, and cried some more.

"I am getting married soon and am getting confused because of you! You who can't bloody get over a aaloo parantha." And she sobbed some more. I was really confused now. I was hungry, had a ton of work to finish, was dead sleepy, but the biggest problem was that I had an engaged woman sitting next to me telling me that she liked me. I seriously did not know what to do. I liked Pooja but I did not want to get into this mess. I did not like her *that* much and I was pretty comfortable out of the troubled situation she was trying to get me into. Had she been married, a fling would have been fine, I had always fantasised that. But this was dangerous, she was engaged and confused as to whether she should marry that guy or not. So I just sat there, looking at my food which would not taste half as good now, and hearing her cry.

She stopped after around five minutes and got up. "Let's go." I knew I had lost all control as soon as she had started crying. I paid the waiter and got up not knowing how my work would finish, how my stomach would get filled and when finally would I get home and lay my back on the bed. Everything was under her control now. We went to her car and Pooja started with her story.

Pooja had what you would call the ideal relationship, until I came into the scene that is. She had known Rannvijay, her boyfriend and then her fiancé for 13 years and they had been dating for the last four. He was what every girl would want in a guy, well educated, earning well etc etc. Everything was perfect, until he proposed.

Pooja said that she had this feeling of being trapped since the time she had gotten engaged. Rannvijay, who until then used to trust her, had started questioning her whereabouts. He wanted to know where she was going, with whom she was going, why was she going and all other related questions a possessive boyfriend asks. Then one day, he told her to leave her job after getting married.

This was the early 2000s, this was not the time you tell a girl what to do or what not to do. Pooja could not believe that it was the same guy who had loved her for the last four years and how all of a sudden, getting engaged to him had changed everything. She could not understand how all of a sudden her independence was being taken away from her. She tried to talk to her mother, then his mother, but no one seemed to understand what she was going through. They just said that there are certain compromises that need to be made to make a marriage successful and her leaving her job was one of them. He anyways made enough money for the both of them and she could sit at home and take care of other things.

That is when she met me. She told me that it wasn't love at first, mainly because I was not that good looking to fall in love at first sight.

She said this in such a matter of fact tone that it really did hurt but I let it pass.

She told me that she started liking me when we got talking. She liked my carefree attitude in life, but she loved the way I could transform myself and give a 100% while at work. That was the first time she used the word love. She said she loved that I could adapt myself according to the situation and behave in the manner required. That is what she had apparently wanted from her guy and had thought that she had found it in Rannvijay but then she started sobbing about how wrong she had been. I had to comfort her but I did not know how. Then, she started sobbing on my shoulder.

We by the way, in the middle of this conversation had walked away from the dhaba and were sitting in her car. A Maruti Alto, in the parking of the building where I worked. It was now 11 pm and a guard walked upto the car and looked inside. He recognised me, faked a salute, put on a mischievous smile and left. I knew what people would be discussing over cigarettes tomorrow. I got my mind back to the problem on hand, on shoulder in fact.

I liked Pooja. She was pretty, she was smart, and she was pretty much better than the best girl I could have managed for myself. But as she had mentioned, for all matters not related to work, I was a pretty chilled out carefree guy and I did not want to get into this mess.

It was a horrible mess. Sure, she gave me the jibbers the other day, and made me appreciate rain, and birds, and grass, but that was when I thought we would go out on a couple of dates and see where it would head from there. Now was very different. Now I was the 'other man' in the relationship. I was not really sure whether I wanted to be the 'other man'. In fact, I was pretty sure that I did not want to be the other man. Just then she left my shoulder, a wet patch on it due to the tears smeared with some of her black kajal. What is it with girls and kajal? She actually was crying.

"So what do we do now?"

So there it was, I was now officially the 'other man'. The 'What do we do now?" had sealed it. Instead of "What do I do now?" it was "What do we do now?" The dreaded word "we".

And then to seal it, she kissed me, right there and then. And I did not resist. It is really difficult to resist when a pretty girl is kissing you. In that Maruti Alto that day, I kissed my carefree life good bye.

I spent the night talking to Pooja saying the usual things a guy says to a girl in order to make her smile. I cracked stupid jokes so that she could smile while she was still sobbing, I made faces, called her names and did all that stuff until finally it was time for her to go home. She lived alone by the way but dropped me first at my place and then went to hers. I did not know whether it was too early to invite her to my apartment. I thought that I was already in the mess so might as well enjoy it. But sense prevailed and she left. Getting out of a kiss was easy, getting out of a night together would have been much more difficult.

As I was walking up the stairs to my one bedroom apartment, I thought about Pooja. She was nice. Had it not been for the engagement angle, I would have been floored if she had fallen for me. But now things were different. The other guy did not even know I existed and here I was, kissing his fiancé. I felt bad for him, and I did not know what I felt for myself. But I really did like her. I had enjoyed the time we had spent together (leaving out today) and whenever I was with her, I wanted time to just stand still.

I unlocked my door, lay on my bed and went to sleep, leaving the decision to another day. Just then my mobile phone beeped. An SMS.

"Gud nite. Thank you. We will make this work J"

The decision had been made, by her. I just had to be a part of the game now. I closed my eyes and tried to sleep, and did manage to in the next 30 seconds. The next morning also started with an SMS. But this time it was my boss.

"Hope you finished the pending work yesterday. Have a presentation in 3 hours. See you in the office."

Oh shit, I had completely forgotten about work. Then the phone beeped again. This time it was her.

"Gud mrng sweetie. Getup now. Time to goto work J"

I actually smiled. Her SMS did make me feel better. I forgot about what was going to happen at work and happily went into the toilet to get ready. Life was good. I had a brand new girlfriend.

The work problem was somehow averted and I met Pooja in the evening at the same cafe where we had met a few days ago when I thought she was not engaged and had tried to win her over. Things were a little different now. I reached early again and ordered the 60 bucks coffee and sat down reading the newspaper. And then I saw her come in again and my heart skipped a beat just like the last time. She was beautiful. I had to make this work.

I saw a gamut of emotions from her over the next few days. At times she would be thrilled to be with me while at others she would be so guilty. Her marriage was in two months and then she would start planning with me on how to end it with her fiancé. It really used to get weird when he used to call her when Pooja and I were on a date. She would receive the call and talk to him all lovey dovey while holding my hand and would expect me to understand.

But I did not. I really did not know where this was headed. If she did break up with Rannvijay, or whatever that guy's name was, I assumed she would expect me to marry her pretty soon as she was apparently ready to get married. I was in no sense ready. Plus I did not know how my parents would react to her. Since the time I had started earning, I had told them infinite times to come to Delhi and live with me. I made enough to run the house now. I know it would have curbed my freedom, but they were my parents and I wanted to take care of them. But they had always rejected the idea saying that they were very well settled in the small little town where they had lived their entire life and did not wish to shift to the madness of Delhi.

I did not know how they would react to me marrying a girl who had recently broken off her engagement. And their opinion really mattered to me. The constant tussle in my life, more so in hers, continued until one day when she called me in office. She said that she was ready. Was ready to tell her parents, his parents, and him, that she was breaking the engagement.

She asked me if she had my support. I knew she wanted more than that, she wanted a commitment.

Just then my boss called me from his cabin urgently and I had to hang up. I knew not giving her the answer she wanted to hear would cost me bad. I walked to my boss's room.

"Pack your bags, you have to goto US this Monday. In four days. I hope all your visa etc work is done."

"But sir, that was not for another 2 months. I had to go in February. Plus, who works in the US in December."

"That is why we are sending you there now. Our American staff will be on leave and you will have to fill in. I hope everything is in order. Visa and all."

"Yes sir."

"Great, contact Saumya, she will get your tickets done."

"Yes sir."

"And son, cheer up please. Whenever I have told anyone that they are going to US, it is usually accompanied by a big thank you, a hug, maybe even chocolates for my kids, a tie for me and a perfume for my wife. You always wanted to goto US. Live your dream."

I smiled. He was a nice guy and he really liked me for the work I had put in for the company. "I will. Thank you, sir."

I would be in the US for six months atleast and Pooja was getting married in around a month and a half now. Things had to be decided in the next 4 days. I went to Saumya to get my tickets done. She booked me on a Saturday instead of a Sunday. 3 days now.

USA had always been my dream destination. In the last couple of years I had resigned from my company a couple of times but both times I was told that I would be sent to the US soon and that very hope made me carry on. I think it is a very natural thing for a person who has come out of a small town in India. First to come to the big city, and then to goto the mightiest country of them all- USA. It was only a couple of months back that my boss had told me that it had finally happened. That finally I was going to goto the United States. In fact, it was the day before I met Pooja for coffee. The day everything had changed.

I had thought that when the day to finally goto US would come I would be thrilled to the bone. I would jump, I would laugh, I would not know how to emote. And the day was finally here. I was not jumping, I was not laughing, but one thing was the way I expected it to be- I did not know how to emote. I called Pooja after getting the tickets done.

"I have to go."

"Where? To your hometown to get your parents so that things can be decided and finalised?"

"No. I have to go far. Remember I told you my company was sending me to the States."

"Yes. But that was like after 4 months, wasn't it?"

"The plan has changed. I have to leave in another 3 days. I have a ticket booked on the Saturday flight."

There was a long silence. Even though we were on other sides of the phone, the awkwardness and uneasiness was palpable. "We need to talk. Meet me at the cafe in an hour."

"But I have a million things to take care of here at office. I am going away for 6 months for heaven's sake. There are office formalities, visa formalities, ticket formalities ..."

"Meet me at the cafe in an hour."

"Okay" After she hung up, I shouted on the phone "Bye!"

I told my boss that I had some US visa related issue and excused myself from the office. I reached the cafe ten minutes early again and ordered the sixty bucks coffee again. The coffee made me smile. I was going to the land where this concept of a cafe had originated with Starbucks. Very soon, I would be having coffee in the country where such cafes had a future, unlike India where they would shut shop soon. Very soon I would be having coffee at Starbucks.

It was the first time the feeling of going to US had sunk in. Just then, Pooja entered. She always looked beautiful in this cafe and always made me change my mind. I was willing to let go of US for her. It was decided. I would tell my boss that I cannot go due to personal reasons. No one questions you when you say 'personal reasons'. Surprisingly, Pooja was not looking as angry as I had expected her to be. She ordered her usual 100 bucks coffee and sat down.

"I have decided what we have to do. And you going to US on Saturday only helps things."

So it was decided, I was not using the 'personal reasons' excuse. I was actually going to US.

"I have known Rannvijay for a very long time. I cannot break his heart."

She said this and looked at me. I did not know how to react. I took a sip of my coffee and tried to cover my face with the mug. Was she going to leave him, or was she going to leave me?

"So, what I will do is that I will break up with him, but will fake a reason." I did not understand how that would not break his heart. "I will not say that I am breaking up with him because I have found you. I will make some 'I am not ready for marriage' type of excuse. So in this way, his ego will not get hurt that he was dumped because of some other guy. And plus, you will be in US, so even if he tries to find out, he will never know that you are the reason."

She had a smile on her face after telling me about her little devious scheme. It seemed like a plan to me because I was not at all involved in the ugly part. I did not have to get married to her then and there. She wanted to wait for sometime so that Rannvijay's ego was not hurt. It really did work well for me. I did not need to involve my parents, did not need to get involved with her or Rannvijay's parents. I could just be a silent spectator.

"And yes, today is the day I am telling Rannvijay that I am breaking up with him. And then, I have a very special treat lined up for you."

She said this, smiled, and left. I smiled. I had a 'very special treat' waiting for me, I was going to the US and I was headed away from all this mess. Life was good. Life was brilliant.

The treat did not happen by the way. After she told Rannvijay, things got pretty ugly between them and then the families. Pooja's parents did not know who to support. It was her fault after all and they were completely unaware of the real reason. Some unpleasant things were said between both the families and all in all, it was not something pretty.

My parents, by the way, had come to see me off. My bags were packed, my mother helped me a lot in doing that, my documents were in order in a pouch clinging to my waistline, I put a jacket around my shoulders, and I was ready to go. My parents dropped me off at the airport and when I was leaving, I could see tears in their eyes. I remembered the day I had left for hostel the first time. There were lots of tears then but as time went by, they gradually understood. Even though I had lived away for a good eight years now, they felt that I was atleast still in the country. Now, I was going far away, into a land they had only heard of. The whole thing got to me and a tear trickled down my cheek as well. Hari was also there to see me off. This had certainly been made into a big deal. I gave him a big hug and asked him to be there in case my parents needed anything. He asked me not to worry. I knew I could trust him on that. We gave our hugs and said our goodbyes and I entered the International airport in Delhi ready for my first international flight, to the United States of America.

It had now really sunk in.

I took a trolley for my luggage and I was adjusting the laptop when I saw Pooja running frantically around the airport. I called out for her. "Pooja, here."

Seeing her did make me feel nice. I did not want to leave without seeing her. She saw me and ran towards me. We hugged.

"How did they let you in this far? This is a high security area."

"How on earth is that important? Don't ask stupid questions. I know people at the airport. Do you know what all is happening at home?"

"I can only imagine it is not pretty."

"Not pretty, it is like a war between the two families."

Then she started crying a little. Then the cry changed to a smile and then laughter.

"What happened?"

"It's just that I have cried so much over the last three days, that now when I am with you, I just want to laugh."

I took her in my arms. "Don't you worry. I will be there for you." She hugged me even tighter. Very soon it was time for her, and more importantly me, to go. I had a flight to catch. We said our goodbyes and again there were some tears. This time, only from her side.

As I was passing through the security check, I realised what I had just done. I had just committed to her.

I was based in New Jersey in USA, across the Hudson river from New York, just like infinite other Indians. It had now been 2 months and I was kind of over the initial hoopla of the huge buildings, and the doughnut and coffee breakfast in the subway, and the fast moving multicoloured people on the street who always seemed to be in a hurry to get somewhere, and the tourists at Times Square, and the strip clubs, and the Broadway, and the big fancy cars and the short dresses even in winters.

I had kind of gotten used to it all by now, plus I lived in a place where there were more Indians than in India. While earlier, I would look back at a pretty girl in tight clothes, I would now not even pass a second glance. It had become as common as a woman wearing a salwaar kameez in India.

Office in US was also the usual. The usual American style and not Indian. More than half the staff was Indian and more than 75% of the work got done in India. There was the usual bickering about bosses, promotions, salary increments etc which we had in India but the duration of the breaks used to be much smaller. People always lived in the fear of being fired and that meant that when they were at work, they would be working, or atleast pretending to. But they were sticklers of time. 9 to 5 meant 9 to 5. They did not enter a minute early and did not leave a minute late. No matter if there was a deadline which was not being met, they all left sharp at 5 unlike us in India who were always willing to do that little extra. But this on time thing made me real bored and lonely.

I had grown up on the small streets of a little town in India and had spent my youth in Delhi and had spent my office time there too. We would go for an hour cigarette break at 7, come back at 8, look at the computer and leave. There was a schedule to it. Here, people were too busy in their own lives to care. People in Delhi knew me and I knew them. It was somehow a little difficult to make friends in the US. I managed some acquaintances with who I could go out for a drink, but not friends with who I could talk nonsense afterwards. People were too busy with their own lives. And the weekends were the worst. I knew nobody in the city and almost every weekend ended up spending a fortune calling my parents, Hari or Pooja back home. I think I wanted to go back. I was not sure. The money here was great, the standard of living was better and I was being offered a one year extension by my company. Maybe I would get used to it. I hoped I would get used to it. This was after all USA, every young man's dream destination.

Things with Pooja were getting steady. The initial hulla regarding Rannvijay had settled and when I told her that my company was open to give me an extension, and that if I wanted, I could very easily find another job and settle here, she kind of got excited. She also harboured the dream of living in the US and it seemed to be coming true through me.

It was during one of the weekends that a ghazal maestro from India was going to perform at one of the auditoriums. I loved his songs and bought the tickets to the concert the day they started selling. Plus, such things really helped kill time when you are feeling all sad and lonely.

The concert was on a Saturday night. I got ready, put on my jacket and reached the place and occupied a seat in the fourth row from the front ten minutes before the show. The hall was completely full. Apparently, I was not the only lonely person in the city. Five minutes later the curtains were raised and the choir was already seated. And then, the maestro himself made an entry. He was dressed in a simple kurta and had a very simple and satisfied happy look on his face, something which was missing in all the people who had come to watch him. In the center of the stage were cushions where he sat down in front of a harmonium and spoke into the mic.

"Namaskar."

The whole place erupted with applause. It was as if he was a rockstar had broken his guitar. He smiled some more. His smile somehow made me feel at home.

"Thank you for all the love that you people have showered on me....." Just then, I saw someone in the choir.

She was in a white dress. She was fair, had a dimpled chin which gave a something special to her smile, long eyelashes, curly at the end, like a princess would want them, kajal around her eyes, kajal to keep away the bad omen from her beautiful face, a small parrot nose, which twitched when she frowned, and black flowing hair, which I would later know, she thought were brown.

It was Shalini.

Just then the maestro started singing "Chandi jaisa rang hai tera, sone jaise baal....." and all of a sudden, nothing else mattered. It all made sense.

The rest of the evening passed in a haze. I could not take my eyes away from her and was completely lost in the mesmerizing beauty of her face coupled with the soulful music running through my ears. Not once did she look at me, I don't think she even noticed me sitting there. After all, there were more than 500 people in the auditorium and plus the last time we had met had been 7 years ago. I had put on 13 kgs since then.

The maestro kept on singing song after song and somehow I could relate all the beautiful lyrics to my life. And then the show ended and before I had a chance to do anything, the curtains went down on the choir and only the lead singer was on the stage to say the thank yous and bid goodbye. He got up from his cushioned seat and folded his hands in an Indian namaskar. Everyone in the crowd got up on their feet to recognise the amazing talent he was and just then, Shalini walked onto the stage with a cordless mic in her hand for the singer.

Before she handed the mic to the singer, she spoke: "Somebody has misplaced their car keys with a flute as a key ring. Please collect it from the reception before you leave."

She had remembered the flute after all these years- my first gift for her. She had remembered me after all these years.

The last words were said by the singer and the entire audience left. I just kept sitting there, thinking about how much had changed since the last time I had met Shalini, about how awkward things would be when I saw her, talked to her, about what would I say to her which would make us feel that we were never apart.

Five minutes later, after everyone had left, I got up and went to the reception. She was already there, sitting on the table, in a changed dress. She was wearing a sleeve less top, blue jeans, minimal makeup and boots. You could think she was any other Indian girl living in New York.

But for me, she was different. She was Shalini.

I had rehearsed a million times in the last five minutes on how I would say the 'hi' but before I could say anything she spoke.

"Fashionably late, aren't we? Let's go."

And there went the awkwardness. She grabbed her overcoat on the way and I followed her out of the building into the snowy New York night.

"You never called."

"What? You had explicitly asked me not to call you. In fact you had told me that you did not even have a phone at your place."

"Well, somebody had to try harder. Getting a girl's phone number is never easy mister engineer. Or is it mister MBA now?"

"No, still mister engineer. And did you actually want me to call? I mean, why did you not give me your phone number?"

"Wait, when did I say that I wanted you to call? I just said that you never called."

She smiled. I smiled. We continued the walking around the square grids of Manhattan. She spoke.

"So how are you?"

"I was good sometime back. Now I am perfect."

"Oh my God! You and your cheesy lines. I still remember 'the only regret I have that it was not a full moon night when we first met'"

"See, you still remember it, it worked."

"I remembered it because it was cheesy, not because it worked."

"By the way, today is a full moon night."

"Where? I don't see the moon."

I pointed towards a glass window and she saw herself. She kicked me, pretty hard for a girl and we both laughed.

"Some people cannot get over being cheesy, but are too laid back to ask for a phone number."

"You can't blame me for that. I was 17. At 17 you don't know girls have so many layers to them. You just believe what they say. You assume, that they will not seek attention."

She gave me another smile.

"So you think I was seeking attention. And do you know any better now?"

"Moaning on a bus as if you were pregnant. Yes, you were seeking attention."

"I actually was, wasn't I?" And she skipped a few paces in front of me.

"I love this city. It has such a feel to it."

"Yeah, not bad. I like snow."

She bent down, made a couple of snowballs and threw them at me.

"One for saying you like New York just for the snow and the other for not following me to the station when I was leaving."

"But I did follow you till the station!"

"Oh yes, I forgot. But I clearly remember how you got down on your knees after the train past."

She got down on her knees on the road in case I had forgotten what I had done.

"So you saw me? Why didn't you wave back?"

"What was the point, you did not even have my phone number!" She said this and threw another snowball at me.

"You are very difficult to understand."

"Stop trying."

"Who said I was?"

She came closer to me, looked me in the eyes. Then she came closer and whispered in my ear.

"Your eyes."

And then she skipped away onto the road. We were walking along the Hudson river and she saw a bench and sat there. I followed her. Her tone changed from the playful to a little more serious but I was not sure. We both sat on the bench, around two feet apart. The New York skyline covered in white snow behind us, the Hudson river in front and some 50 storey high buildings of New Jersey beyond, which somehow did not feel that big in front of the behemoth at Manhattan. There were some boats on the river and it was as picturesque a scene as it could have been in New York.

"Don't you just love it here?"

"I have been here only for two months."

She continued. "Oh! That's it? But just look in front of you. On the back you have all what man could have achieved- huge buildings, billions of dollars of trade, the whole world's economy is governed right here, right behind us. And then you have this river, which majestically runs in between the two cities dividing them and telling them that nature doesn't really care what you make."

"What? I don't get what you are saying."

"Honestly, neither do I. I wanted to make a statement about how this city has been able to put together nature and man's development. But I don't think I really was able to put forth the sentiment."

"You weren't."

"I know. It got lost in the words somehow. But you get what I mean."

"I get what you mean. But don't really understand. Honestly, I don't see much of nature in this city. Concrete jungle is what I was told it is, and a concrete jungle is what I see."

"Shut up. Don't you get it. 'Concrete' as in manmade, and 'jungle' as in natural?"

"Are you drunk?"

"I could have been if someone had offered me a drink."

"Was I supposed to?"

"No, just like you weren't supposed to ask for my number. Now sit here, I have to go and pee."

"Out here in the open?"

"Very funny."

She left for a public restroom and I sat alone, looking at the huge river in front of me. There were personal boats of people out in the water. The whole city seemed so alive at 1 am at night. Maybe she did have a point when she said that it was man and nature's best creation. She came back.

"So, you understand what I say?"

"Kind of. But leave it. Tell me, how come you are here, what did you do in music, how long have you been in this city. There is so much to catch up on and here you are talking arbit gyaan."

She smiled, but this time, it was not in the eyes. We sat on the bench, a one foot distance between the two of us.

"I just followed my heart. And my heart brought me here. You tell me how come you are here. I mean I know it fits into your secure life and future theory but please tell me that there is more to it? Please tell me that you are here on a secret mission to find aliens and that the aliens are going to invade the earth and you are going to save all of us."

I could sense she was trying to change the topic of discussion from me to her. I smiled and let her.

"I stopped living that dream of saving the earth when I was eight. No, there is absolutely nothing more to it. I passed out of college, got a decent job, got sent here on a project and have been here for the last few months. Simple as that. And completely according to plan."

"So what comes next? A wife, kids, car, a home, a dog, a cat, a kennel, a whatever in which a cat lives?"

"Hahaha, no, what comes next is a moment that takes my breath away."

"And my only regret in life still stays. Why did I not throw you out of the train the first day we met? You and your cheesy dialogues!!"

We both looked at each other with a little giggle on our lips. This time, the smile reached her eyes. I tried to shift the topic again.

"Enough about me. You tell me. A small town girl living in the US, US clothes, a put on US accent. What happened there?"

"First of all, there is no put up US accent. And it is not even called US accent, it's called American accent. Dumb ass. And what do you mean by US clothes? What do you expect me to wear at this temperature? A navel exposing saree?"

She saw the mischief in my eyes. "Don't answer that?"

"No matter what you say, I still will. Yes, I want to see you in a navel exposing saree."

"Happy that you have said it?"

"Pretty much made my day."

"So out of all that has happened so far, saying these lines has made your day?"

"Nothing has happened so far!!"

"And nothing will!!"

"But seriously, how come you are here?"

"Why can't I be?"

"A question as an answer to a question is not really helping."

"Okay, so let me start. Since the last time we met. So that time, I loved singing. Now come to the present, I still love singing, and, I kind of get paid for it. Not much, but enough. I had grandiose dreams of making it big as a singer, but I could not. So here I am, singing in a choir."

That was the first time I saw a tinge of sadness, or remorse in her eyes which came down to her voice. I felt it was something more than what she had just said. She continued.

"I know you will say that time is still on my side. That I am 24. But when you know you are not good enough, then it really does not matter how old you are, does it?"

I didn't know what to say. She was the girl who had inspired me to have a dream seven years ago. To look within and see what I really wanted to do in life. I didn't do it was a different matter altogether but I had expected atleast her to do it. I had counted on her to do it. If she could not achieve what she wanted to in music, then people like me were good in following other rats in the rat race.

She sensed the awkwardness which had stepped into our conversation for the first time. And then she burst out laughing.

"Hahahaha."

She got up from the bench and started jumping and moving her head all around.

"Hahahaha. Got you didn't I? What do you think, only you can speak movie dialogues? I my friend can do so to. All I said was crap. Basically, I am still training to be a singer and got a chance to sing in the choir of the maestro himself. Who would let such an opportunity go by?"

What she said now was making sense. Singing in the choir of the great ghazal singer was indeed a big deal if you were an aspiring singer. But I was not sure whether she was acting earlier or was acting now. The spark in her eyes was just not there, but I did not press. And the dancing and the head banging really made it look like a put up act. She might be a good singer, but she was not a good actor. I stayed out of the success part of it and tried to change the topic.

"Tell me. What would you have done had I kissed you on the top of the rock in Delhi?"

"I would have liked it. It was such a romantic place. I just wish I had a romantic guy with me. The guy who was with me did not even take my number."

"Would you let that go please!"

"Sorry, won't repeat the fact that you did not take my number again." She giggled. I tried to get close.

"You are seven years too late buddy. A New York skyline cannot meet the romanticism of a Delhi winter morning."

"But I was scared at that time. I thought you would slap me."

"I was ready that time. I might slap you now. Too bad, isn't it?"

She smiled some more.

"You know what, even I don't want to kiss you now."

"Still scared?"

"Maybe I have better options."

She held my hand, looked down and said "Really."

I knew she was trying to get me. I stood ground. "Yes, really."

She looked up and I saw the passion in her eyes once more. Maybe this time it was for me. She came close. I puckered my lips. She started laughing again and mocked me.

"Yeah really Shalini. I don't want to kiss you. I have better options now. No Shalini. Don't take advantage of me Shalini. Please let me goo."

Then suddenly she stopped and came closer to me again. My lips puckered again and she started laughing again.

"You guys. All are the same."

"Have quite bit of an experience, do you?"

"I have had my share of fun."

"How much fun?"

"That is for you to think of."

A huge ferry passed from in front of us. There was an open party going on in the ferry. A bachelor party I would assume as there were girls in the smallest of clothes gyrating to songs in the cold winter.

"All you guys are the same. Atleast keep your mouth closed when you are gawking."

"I wish all girls were the same and were like those exotic dancers there."

She playfully hit me on my hand and there was silence. The same silence which we had accepted when we had first met. The silence did not make it awkward even this time. After around five minutes of sitting on the bench, looking at the river, she admiring the beauty of the place and me of the girls, she said "Let's go for another walk."

"Let's just sit. Don't worry, I am just looking at those girls. I am thinking only about you."

"What a coincidence. I am looking at the guys and I am also thinking about me. How I would love to dance 'exotically' for them on that boat. But here I am sitting on this bench with you."

"Are you sure you are not drunk. Are you sure they did not mix anything in your water?"

"I wish they had. Atleast I could have done things which I cannot do now that I am sober."

I raised my eyebrow. "And what might that be madame? You can always pretend you are drunk."

"I told you , that I want to dance for those guys."

"Can I watch sitting here when you are dancing for them on that ferry?"

"You are so bloody cheap."

We both looked into each other's eyes and the eyes smiled. I was enjoying this directionless conversation with her. But then she got it a direction.

"Are you happy?"

I tried to keep the conversation light.

"Yes, I am sitting with a beautiful girl and watching some more beautiful girls dance. Life could not have been better."

I looked towards her and this time she was serious. I also took the same route.

"I don't know. I don't think in that way. There was nothing that I really wanted, so you can look at it in two ways. Either what I have got means everything to me, or whatever I have got doesn't really matter that much. Honestly, the secure future, engineering, maybe MBA later, were all dreams my parents harboured for me and I guess by mistake, I thought they were my dreams as well. But as time went by, I realised they weren't. And as time went by, I realised that I did not have any dreams. So, the question of them being fulfilled, of me being satisfied or happy never really comes to my mind. I find the work I do at office mind numbingly boring at times while at other times I find it ok. It does not really involve brains. You just have to settle into a system. But I am honest with my work. At the end, it is my work for which I get paid for. It is my work which lets me enjoy the lazy weekends, the parties, the fun. And yes, I feel good when I am with friends. So if you ask me if I am happy, I will say I don't know. Maybe because there are no unique milestones set in life, reaching which would give me happiness. I have the usual needs and wants- when do I buy a car next, when do I buy a home and all such things. But so many people around you are already doing all that so when you end up doing it too, it kind of loses importance."

"Hmm."

"I mean, when I was 17, I had thought that if by 25 I make a certain amount of money, life would be set and I would be the happiest man. Today, I make twice as much as that money but it doesn't really seem to matter.

"Hmm"

"I say all that long story. Give you insights into my life which even I was not sure about till now, and all I get is a 'hmm'."

She lightened the mood a little.

"You want a kiss."

"I am not falling for it this time."

This time she puckered her lips and came close to me. The distance between us reduced from one feet to 6 inches, to 2 inches. She whispered.

"I heard in a movie that a guy has to cover 80% of the distance between two lips. If the girl wants, she will cover the remaining 20. But here I am already done with 80%."

I closed my eyes and puckered up for the third time. And she started laughing.

"All guys are the same."

"I open my heart out and this is what I get. Ridicule."

"No, go on. I am listening."

"Naa, you spoilt the moment."

"Go on!"

"Okay. So what I was saying was that 'are you happy' does not have a definite answer for me. 'I don't know' is the answer to that question. At times, I am satisfied, at times I am longing for more. I guess that is happiness right. Being satisfied, but yet wanting to grow?"

"I don't think so. If you are not sure whether you are happy or not. I think you are not happy then."

"But I know I am not sad. And what is that euphoric feeling I will get if I am happy? Does Sachin Tendulkar still feel like the happiest person in the world when he comes out to bat every time?"

"Why do guys relate everything to cricket?"

"Because that is what we understand. We also relate everything to girls, but then, some girls would not even reciprocate, so we have to fall back on our ally, cricket."

"I will ignore what you just said and will reply on the cricket part. So, yes, I think Sachin does feel like the happiest person when he comes out to bat every day. That is why he is so great at what he does."

"But doesn't even he have unfulfilled dreams. Even he has not lifted the world cup."

"Happiness does not mean not having unfulfilled dreams. It means that you are working towards those dreams. And you bet one day he will lift that cup."

"I think so too, hope it happens in 2007 only."

"I guess it won't happen now, it will happen later. I predict 2011."

"As you say madame. I have anyways considered you to be the last authority on all worldly matters."

"How on earth is what I just said gyaan?"

"Yeah, it's not. Leave that. You tell me miss philosophical, are you happy?"

"Well, I am thinking about dancing exotically in front of men in bare minimum clothes on a snowy New York night. I am not happy. I am thrilled!"

"Cut it, seriously, are you happy?"

She looked me in the eyes and again she had that serious look, that hollow look.

"I told you I am not happy. I will also tell you that I am not thrilled either. But I am not sad. I am in a state of indifference. And that is a worse state than being sad."

This time I knew that the sentence would not be followed by any laughter. But she smiled. A sad smile. An indifferent smile.

"May I ask what happened?"

"You may ask. But I may not tell."

"Hmm."

"Okay. This is something I have never told anyone. In fact, I may tell you things tonight which I might not have owned to myself."

I tried to lighten the mood.

"Like that you want to kiss me right now?"

I did a goofy smile.

"Yes."

She just said that which such a straight face. I did not know how to react. Luckily for me, she continued.

"I want to kiss you, make love to you right now but like everything else in life, I am scared of failure. I am scared that I may never see you again after this, that this might be the first and only time we make love, that you will forget me one day."

She had a stoic face devoid of emotion. I did not know whether this was an invitation or whether it was abdication. She continued speaking.

"Music ditched me, and I feel that just like music, everything else will. And just like I have been trying to follow music even now, I will try to follow love, and just like I have never been able to achieve music, I will never be able to achieve love."

I could not understand what was going on. The past few hours I had spent with her, she had seemed to be the most carefree and independent girl I had met. I could have never guessed that there was such a deep layer to her as well.

"So what had happened? Last time we met, you were so passionate about music and about being a singer. What changed that?"

"Nothing, as I mentioned earlier, I just realised that I was not good enough. And when you realise that whatever you have been dreaming for your entire life has been worthless, then life looses all purpose and meaning."

"But what happened? I heard you sing and you were pretty good."

"That was seven years ago. Things changed after that."

"Why? What happened?"

"It was not one event, it was a series of events which changed everything. And after a time, I just did not feel like singing anymore. In fact, that is the reason I am here. My mother made me leave the country because everything in India reminded me that I had been a failure. That I had done something which I probably should not have. But I don't regret doing it."

"But you are just 24. What could have happened that changed everything so suddenly?"

"My father died. And I guess, that just changed everything. I think I thought that I had failed in life, that in fact, life had failed me. Nothing mattered after that, all of a sudden, not even music. And by the time I got back to it, even the music had died. I don't even know why I am telling you all this. Maybe because I have not talked to anyone about it, maybe because I want to get it out of my system and move on in life. That is what I have been trying to do in my life for the past few years. I am trying to move away from music, to move away from my father's death, am trying to find a new life in this new city. But I am not sure whether running away from it is the answer, or running towards it is. So at times I try to sing, just to prove to myself that I can, like I did in this show. And at times, I am so completely switched off from it, that I feel as if I never sang."

She looked into the vast expanse of the river in front of us as she was speaking. She was just staring, at nothing in particular, but I knew, she was remembering her childhood.

"My father died two years after I met you, and I guess I have still not been able to get over it. Don't ask me how. After that, I lost all interest in life, all my confidence. A father is supposed to be a little girl's hero, but when you realise that your hero is actually not who you wanted him to be, you start doubting everything else you believe in life as well. I remember what had happened to my mother after his death. To me, nothing made sense. Music was the last thing on my mind at that time. I was just in college, I had started performing in shows, I had started making a mark, but everything changed after that. I just realised that I could not have what I loved. I could not have my life, and I could not have music. And since that time, I have lost complete faith in everything. I have lost faith in myself. And I am not even sure if I regret it."

She continued staring into nothing. I saw a tear slide down her cheeks. She wiped it and changed modes, tried a fake smile.

"Leave all that. Got a little too much didn't it."

"Can you sing for me?"

"What?"

"Can you sing for me. Just for me. I will not say that it is good, I will not say that it is bad. I just want you to sing for me. Once. Please."

"You and your filmy ways."

"Please. You know I want to say things like 'don't worry, things will be fine' but you know when people say that, they actually mean that things will not be fine and that you have to learn to live with it. I will not say any such thing. All I am asking you to do is sing for me."

She smiled, and this time the smile reached the eyes. She got up and stood in front of me.

"Okay, I will sing a song from a hindi movie. I try to stay away from music these days, but, I just can't."

"Now shut up with the gyaan and start singing."

"It's from a movie- Zakhm with Ajay Devgan in it."

"I am not interested in the details. Just sing."

"Tum aaye to aaya mujhe yaad,

Gali me aaj chand nikla"

And she sang the full song.

She ran towards me and hugged me and started crying. I just put her head on my shoulder and let her. Maybe it was because she was lonely, maybe it was because she felt she was close to me, or maybe because it had been long overdue, but she trusted me and cried in my arms. After around five minutes she let go of me.

"I am sorry. I don't know why I did this. You are the first person who I have told about my life. In fact, you are the first friend I have met since I have come to this country. Thank you."

I said nothing, just smiled. This was difficult on her. I did not want to make it worse.

"Let's go."

She said this and took charge, we were off again. In the square streets of Manhattan, out in the cold at 3 am on a Saturday night.

"Most places here open till 4, I will take you to a place which opens till 7."

We stopped a passing cab and she said "42nd Street Broadway please."

The cab driver was an Indian and said "Ji Madam ji" and he got us there in fifteen minutes. She tipped him a dollar. He was happy.

We entered into a pub like what I had never seen before. There were seven different parts to the pub. One was playing retro, one jazz, one contemporary, and the other parts some other kind of music. I think there was a strip club as well. But the only thing common was that people were drinking and people were dancing. Shalini took my arm and took me straight to the bar.

"Two Jager Bombs please."

I had been in New York for almost two months and I had not heard of this drink. Maybe I was hanging out with the wrong set of people. The barman took two shot glasses and poured Jagermeister – a drink made of 56herbs and spices- into them. He then opened a Red Bull can and poured half the content into a beer glass and the remaining half into another beer glass. He then handed us the shot of Jager and the beer glass with the Red Bull. I looked at Shalini confused as to what to do with it.

"So ready?"

"Not really. I don't know what to do."

"Don't tell me you have not had a Jager Bomb ever? You have been in New York for more than two months! What's wrong with you? Did you come here to listen to Indian ghazals on a Saturday night or did you come here to have fun."

She was practically shouting, it was so loud with the blaring music. I shouted back.

"I guess you are right. From tomorrow, I will hang out with you."

She ignored what I said.

"So what you do is, you drop this shot glass into the beer glass with the Red Bull in it. The contents mix, but don't wait for them to mix, and then you gulp it down in one go."

"In one go? Are you crazy? What is the alcohol content in this?"

" That's the good part. Pretty much! So here we go."

She gave me my shot glass and the beer glass.

"On India okay. One, two, Indiaaaaaa."

I dropped the shot glass and gulped down the mixture in one go. It was the best drink I had ever had. My hands went up in the air.

"One more."

"One more."

After 4 more Jager Bombs, we were high and were on the dance floor swaying to the beats, swaying to the music, swaying to each other.

"Let's goto the strip club."

"But you are a girl!"

"But you are a guy. Why are you saying no?"

"Valid point. Let's go!"

I had been to strip clubs before but never had it been as much fun. After around three and a half hours in that place, completely drunk, happy and crazed out, we both came out singing- "Gali me aaj chaand nikla, gali me aaj chand nikla" We got to the metro station. Now was the bad part, I had to drop her home but I was sure this time we would meet again. There was one train standing headed to somewhere in New York and one headed to New Jersey. She said she lived in New York so she would take one train and I the other one to New

Jersey. She gave me her cell phone number. But I insisted that I drop her first. She said ok but that the train currently at the station now did not stop at her stop. So we decided to wait for the next one.

We sat on a bench next to the stationary train. It was very early in the morning and the city was asleep. Just as the doors of the stationary train were about to get closed and it was about to start moving, she ran and got onto the train. And the doors jammed and train started moving. All the haze, all the alcohol suddenly went off my system and I could not get what was going on around me. She was on the other side of the glass, on the other side of the metro, and the train started moving. Our eyes met and I knew that I would not be seeing her again. The train kept on moving, and she kept on going away. I did not know why. I was down on my knees again, just like seven years ago.

Nothing had changed. I took out the slip which had her number on it, the number had one digit short. She did not want to see me again. I had lost her again. I reached home, sobered up and tried to get her contact from the auditorium where she had performed the day before. After cooking up a story that her father had a heart attack I somehow managed to figure out in which hotel the choir was staying. It was a hotel down town. I called them up and asked for Shalini.

"Sir, she checked out one hour ago."

That was it, I had lost her again.

I went into a stupor for the next few days. I did not try to look for her because there was actually no point in doing so. If she wanted to see me again, she would see me again. Running after her or chasing her would not really help. I really wanted to help her, and I guess, that was the reason that she did not want me around. She needed love, not pity. I became very lonely over the next few weeks in that city. The country, which used to be a dream for me, just did not excite me anymore. All I could associate with the city was Shalini and she had gone, she had deserted me. I was having a chat with my mother on one of the days and that is when I broke down. I cried. After 8 years. And cried in front of my mother.

I know Shalini was not the reason for my crying, it was mainly the loneliness, but I did not want to be in US anymore. I wanted to go back home, go back to the place where my friends were, where Pooja was, and where my parents were. I told my office about my decision and they were supportive of it. They were surprised as to why I wanted to leave the land of dreams so soon, but they were supportive. They knew they would not have any trouble getting any of my colleagues to US to fulfil his dream.

I booked a ticket for the next week. I did not tell anyone that I was coming back. I wanted to surprise my parents and Pooja. My parents had anyways been worried sick since the day I broke down and had ordered me to leave everything and come back then and there. When I got the ticket in my hand, things started to look better. There was a longing to go home. I had been here only for 3 months but it seemed like an eternity. I missed my friends, I missed my country, I missed my parents. And then the day came, I was headed back home.

I checked into the airport with my luggage. I had bought quite a few things for Hari, Pooja and my parents and was picking up the compulsory chocolates for my other friends at the Duty Free shop. I boarded the Virgin Atlantic flight to London where I would have a 2 hour stopover. I entered the flight and straight away went into a deep slumber. I was awakened when the flight had a rough landing and we jumped a couple of times on the runaway. There was a cry of relief from everyone as we landed safely. All the flights I had ever been on always had a rough landing. I think it was something to do with me.

Heathrow London is a crazy place. I got off at Terminal 3 gate number 32 and had to walk a whole lot of distance to the main terminal where it would be announced where my next flight would board from. There were two paths, separated by a glass wall. One path was used to goto the main terminal 3 from where further information was received regarding your next flight. The other path was the one which people who had checked in from Terminal 3 would use to goto their flights. There was a glass wall surrounding these two paths. I had got off the plane and was ambling lazily down my path with my laptop in tow looking around at whatever of London I could see. There were ads of Harrods, of Broadway and some other brands which I could barely recognise. I bumped into the guy walking in front of me and decided to look straight. And that was when I saw her, again. And this time, not after seven years.

She was on the other side of the glass wall moving towards a certain gate to catch a flight to a certain city. She was 40 feet away, wearing a simple black dress with an overcoat around her shoulder. She was carrying a trolley with one hand and her purse was on the other. She was now 30 feet away. I shouted her name. Apparently the glass wall was sound proof because everyone on my path looked at me with a crazy look but no one from the other side did. She was now 10 feet away, I shouted again. More stares, but only from my side. 5 feet away. I ran towards the glass wall and banged and some people from the other side looked at me but she did not turn. She kept on walking and went right past me. And then she looked back.

She had seen me all along, I could see it in her eyes. She stopped for a split second, and then continued to some gate to board some flight to some country. I stood there on the glass wall until security came for me. They had apparently seen me banging the partition and had questions to ask.

After spending around an hour of my time in London explaining to the police what I actually was doing, I was let free. My mind was devoid of all emotions. She did not want me in her life. It was pretty clear and evident. But I knew we would meet again. This chance meeting was not the end of our story. I boarded the flight to New Delhi and again fell fast asleep as soon as the plane took off.

I landed at India at around 8 am on a Sunday. I got off the plane and was back in the Delhi chill. I could feel the smell of my country. It felt nice to be back home. The baggage and other details took around 3 hours. Again a characteristic of my country. I thought my baggage had been lost but then I saw it. It was going round and round on a conveyor belt meant for some other flight.

Such things happen in this country.

I got out of the airport and was kind of overwhelmed to see what was happening outside. Mothers were meeting long lost sons, wives were meeting husbands who had gone away to earn more for the family, kids were meeting their fathers after an eon.

There was a movie, Love Actually, in which the narrator says that if you want to see true love, you should go to the arrival of an international airport. He could not have been more spot on. No one had obviously come to greet me, I had not told anyone. But I had a smile nevertheless. Seeing so much love around you does make you feel good. I hired a prepaid taxi to my apartment.

It felt great entering the smelly little place. It felt like home, it was home. I guess there was a dead rat in a corner but that was ok. I stuffed the bags in the place, took a shower, thought of finding the dead rat but let the thought be just a thought, and I was ready to receive all the love I had missed for the past three months.

All of a sudden, there was an excitement to meet Pooja, an excitement which I had honestly never felt before. I was in two minds on whether I had cheated on her but I decided I had not, not atleast physically. And that is what counts. I was now ready to leave Shalini behind and start afresh with Pooja. If Shalini did not want me, to hell with her.

I took a shower and got into new clean clothes, new clean American clothes. There was no sign of jet lag on me. I was in love again. There was a constant whistle in my head as I rummaged through my bags and took out the stuff I had bought for Pooja and left for her place.

Pooja lived around 5 kms from where I lived. She used to live with a roommate but girls usually don't get along together so she moved out and took her own place. Her parents were based out of Chandigarh. I bought flowers on the way and rang the bell with my arms wide open. I heard a voice from inside "They are here."

It was an excited kind of voice. I got a little confused as to what was happening when Pooja opened the door wide and there she was, looking beautiful in a red salwaar suit, her hair hanging around her face and the biggest smile I had ever seen on her.

But then the smile faded, and slowly turned into a scowl.

Behind her I could see a couple who I assumed were her parents and another girl who could have been her friend or her sister.

"What are you doing here?"

"I came back. Just for you. I thought I would surprise you."

"You should have called. You told me you were going on a trip and your phone would be switched off."

"That was because I was on a flight back to India."

The lady from behind called out "Who is it beta? Is it Rannvijay's friend?"

I was shocked. When did Rannvijay, Pooja's ex fiancé come into the picture?

"Pooja, What is happening?"

"You should have called. Please leave now."

"I will not leave, what is going on?"

The lady, her mother, walked up to the door.

"Beta, who is it?"

I was about to tell her my name.

"Aunty I am.."

"Oh my God, you are the one who lead to my little girl's engagement breaking up earlier. How dare you come to our house and that too on such an auspicious day?"

I could not understand what was happening.

"Pooja, what is this lady saying?"

"This lady is her mother and is asking you why on earth are you here? You tried to break my little daughter's marriage with Rannvijay earlier as well but were unsuccessful. Now that we have managed to convince his parents to accept our daughter again, you have again come to spoil everything. What kind of a filthy man are you?"

I looked at Pooja.

"Please tell me this is not true."

Her mother started to speak but I looked at her and she shut up. Pooja spoke.

"I was about to tell you."

I wanted to shout at her, to break things in her house, to punch that Rannvijay, but I did nothing like that. I was unwanted in her life, just Iike I was unwanted in Shalini's. I walked out. Pooja tried calling for me but all was lost. I went to Hari's place. Luckily he was there. He saw me and he knew something was wrong and I broke down for the second time in a week, this time in front of my best friend. And I knew he would understand. We had a long chat that day, Hari and I. About life, just about life. It felt good connecting with him after a long time. I told him that I would take a week off and goto my parents' place and would then join office. I slept the night at his place. In the morning, before I left, he just said one thing

"If I can do anything to make this better for you, I will."

And I knew he meant it, and that really did make it better. There was someone outside my parents who loved me. He would do anything for me.

PRESENT DAY
2011

As the engagement was more of a family affair with no alcohol, atleast no alcohol officially, I had to take my friends out for a drink to celebrate the end of my freedom. It was an only guys night out and Kriti jokingly asked me to stay away from Hari and left to be with her parents. There were 8 of us guys and we went to a new bar which had just opened in Gurgaon. It supposedly had great live music and a great blend of cocktails. We settled into the bar and ordered a round of drinks. All lights then went out and all the focus shifted to the stage. Apparently some locally famous singer from US was playing. She had recently started making a mark on the American stage. The lights went out, and then all of them shone at one bright spot on the stage.

She was in a black dress. She was fair, had a dimpled chin which gave a something special to her smile, long eyelashes, curly at the end, like a princess would want them, kajal around her eyes, kajal to keep away the bad omen from her beautiful face, a small parrot nose, which twitched when she frowned, and black flowing hair, which I would later know, she thought were brown.

It was Shalini.

"Hello India. I have travelled the world, sung in front of people of all countries and continents, but never have I come here and sung in front of my own people. So this is my first time here, and I hope it is as memorable for you guys as it is for me."

She raised a glass, "This is for my people. Cheers."

She downed whatever was in the glass in one neat go and started a fusion song. The music was beautiful, her voice was beautiful, she was beautiful.

The singing continued for two hours. It was not supposed to be a performance, it was supposed to be a live singer at a bar where the music is in the background and everyone is busy with their own conversations and clap at the end. I was supposed to be drinking all the alcohol possible as it was my party with the guys after my engagement. But we all were completely queued into the songs which she was singing. After around two hours, she stopped. I was not even sure if she had seen me. I did not know what to do. Should I go upto her and talk to her? Should I ignore her and forget that I ever saw her again?

These questions were in my head when she took the mic again and said "Before, I leave for a little break. I will leave you with some lines from a pretty old hindi movie which somehow have meant a lot to me."

"Tum aaye to aaya mujhe yaad, gali me aaj chand nikla. Jaane kitne dino ke baad, gali me aaj chand nikla."

"Thank you everyone."

There was a huge round of applause. No matter how sophisticated we want to project ourselves, all Indians prefer a hindi song to any fusion. But that was besides the point.

A drunk Hari looked at me and I knew that he understood. I had told him about the entire episode with Shalini when Pooja had dumped me. He did not say anything. But his eyes told me to let her go. I was now engaged and meeting Shalini could not help me in any possible manner. I looked at him and I guess he could see it in my eyes. I just had to go.

He nodded, I don't know whether in agreement or in disapproval. But whatever it was, he understood. I had to go.

I slipped my engagement ring in my pocket. I did not know why I did that. If Shalini would ask, I would obviously tell her that I had found someone. I would tell her that I could not wait for her when I see her only once in 6 years, I could not wait for her when she had so easily walked out on me, I could not wait for her if she had never wanted me to wait.

I walked out of the bar. I was still not sure whether she had seen me or not. There was nobody in site. Just then I heard "Let's go."

She had a cigarette in her hand, and a small little smile on her face. We left the bar together.

Gurgaon has tried to develop itself as downtown New York with huge buildings, office space, expensive homes and traffic jams. And it has kind of succeeded. But unlike Manhattan, a lively cosmopolitan nightlife does not exist once the office gates are closed. What exists here is a scary uninhabited palace of glass with no one in site. And therein lies the difference and the beauty.

The bar where Shalini was singing and I was drinking with my friends was one of few such places in the Gurgaon corporate parks. We kept on walking in between the huge buildings with the lit up National Highway on one side of us. For ten minutes, there was no conversation between us. Just serene silence. It was not that we did not have anything to say, it was just that there was so much we did not know how to begin. She started.

"Thanks."

"For what?"

"I won't say that whatever little I have achieved is because of you and that night we spent together. But that night helped me get rid of one very important thing. Self doubt."

I gave a sarcastic comment "So is that why you are here again? To let me help you solve some other problems."

She smiled. A genuine one. I could tell from the eyes.

"No, I just wanted to thank you before you started off with the questions. But surprisingly, you started off with sarcasm."

I gave her a smile. One which started with sarcasm but as I looked into those eyes, it transformed to a genuine one.

"Why did you just leave?"

"Because I did not want you to feel that I was a loser."

"But I never felt you were a loser."

"That is because I left before you could think that."

"Wait, I am confused."

She smiled again.

"Chicken and egg isn't it. I was in a pretty bad condition at that point in life. I had met you after 7 years and that meant something to me. We could have stayed in touch and I could have told you how sucky my life is and then instead of excitement, surprise, joy and honestly, a little bit of lust which I see in your eyes today, I would have seen scorn, irritation and the feeling that oh no, not her again. Had we been in touch, I would have just seen pity. I left so that we could meet again. And we have. And I always knew we would."

"First of all, there is no lust in my eyes."

"Does that mean I am not pretty?"

"When did I say that?"

"So that means I am pretty."

"I did not say that either, but yes. You are pretty."

"So you admit, there is a little bit of lust in your eyes."

"Never mind that. What I was saying is that.."

"What you were saying is that I am pretty and you have lusty eyes."

"Shalini!!"

"Okay, sorry. Please continue."

"No. You spoiled the moment. It was such a sweet and deep and emotional moment. And you spoiled it."

"No no no. Let's try again. So you were saying."

"I was saying that.."

"That I am pretty and you are lusty. Hahahahah"

"I am not talking to you."

"Sorry last time. I promise."

"No."

"Please."

"Well, okay. What I was saying is that you have not met me for the last what, 6 years, so that when we meet after six years, that is today, we have a perfect date?"

"First of all, don't get too full of yourself- this is not a date. And second, yes."

"Pretty weird aren't you?"

"Pretty, definitely yes. Weird, yeah, maybe a little."

I touched her hand. Then I held it. She did not shove it away, and neither did she embrace it. We walked, hand in hand, for the first time, in between empty offices in Gurgaon. Silently, both of us taking in the fact what this meant to us. Both of us unsure why it meant so much.

"So after we saw each other in London, and I completely ignored you, did you try to look for me? By the way, did you notice that I did see you?"

"Obviously I knew you saw me. Madam, you are not as subtle as you think. You looked back and our eyes met."

"Damn, I had controlled myself all the way when you were jumping on the other side of the glass."

"Why did you ignore me?"

"I didn't want to hurt you."

"You know right that I am a human being. And human beings are hurt on being ignored. Not on being embraced."

"I know, but I just wanted you to believe that it was not me but someone else you saw. I told you right, at that stage in my life, I could not let you come close to me because I did not want you to feel pity for me."

"So what did you want me to feel?"

"So did you try and look for me?"

"Where could I? I mean, it's not that I would travel all around the world looking for you. I did not even know which country you were in!"

"You mean nothing? You did not try locate me on Facebook, twitter or anything like that?"

"I wanted to. Five years ago, these things were not that popular. And as time went by.."

"As time went by, you forgot me."

"As time went by, I tried to convince myself that I was better off without knowing. That if we had to meet, it would not be through twitter or Facebook. It would be like this."

"Big believer in destiny?"

"You have made me."

Some more silence.

"So honestly, you never looked me up?"

"Okay, I did. But I never found you. In fact, I do it every day. What name are you registered under?"

"My singing name. Shaila."

"Did you ever try to look me up?"

"I am a very strong person. I left you in New York when I needed you the most. I never looked you up. I do believe in destiny. And I knew we would meet."

Some more silence.

"Not even once? I mean, I am pretty easy to find on Facebook. I have a pretty uncommon name."

"Not even once."

I felt a little relief on this. If she had not visited my Facebook page, she did not know I was getting engaged. It made me feel a little relieved and in some time, a little guilty as well. We kept on walking.

"So what made you come back to India?"

"Would it make you happy if I said that you made me come back?"

"I guess it will. But I know better."

"Work. Work made me come back to India. I am decently famous in US now singing fusion music. My manager got me some shows here, so I thought, why not. It had been a long time since I had been here anyways. Not after my mother died."

"I am sorry."

"Don't be. So yes, I am back here for work. Leave that. You tell me. How is your life going? Everything according to plan is it? Good college, good job, good car, good wife?"

"Well, almost on track. I did MBA after we met."

"Good college?"

"Tier one."

"As expected of you."

"So yes, I did MBA, then took up a job. Have been working in the same company ever since. So good college- yes, good job- yes, good car- car can be better."

"And."

"And what?"

"And good wife?"

I put my hands in my pocket and felt the ring.

"I am not married yet. Maybe haven't had the time so far, or maybe haven't found the right person."

"Haha. Right person."

"What is so wrong in 'right person.'"

"Nothing. It's just that 'right person' is so typically you. Everything has to be perfect, doesn't it? Good college, good job, good girl."

"So what is wrong in that?"

"I am not saying there is anything wrong. How about selecting something which is not right for once in life, and then seeing what happens after that?"

"You are weird. I like things the way they are."

"Ok then. So the search for the right girl continues is it?"

"At times yes, at times no. I don't know. Maybe, I have left it to destiny like you have left so many things to it."

I looked down. I was lying, and I did not want her to catch hold of me. I tried to change the topic.

"Life has been pretty much similar to the last time we met. It's just that the job is different, the money is more, but the routine is pretty much the same."

"That's not good is it? That in the last six years, your life has not changed one bit."

"I have gained a few kgs."

"Okay, it's sad that there has been no positive change in your life in the last six years. And I bet you are going to the gym to lose them."

"How did you know? Does it show?" I flexed my muscles to check if it did actually show.

"No you idiot- it does not show *at all*. I knew that you goto a gym because you don't like change. Even if you gain weight, you will like to get back to the stage you were in before."

"Now that you put it that way, it is quite boring. You tell me, what interesting things have you been upto."

"Well, the last time we met, I was in a real low stage in life. But after meeting you, I don't know how, but things changed. It's not that you did wonders or anything, it's just that, I started feeling better again. The confidence was back. When we saw each other at London, that time, I was headed to Paris for an interview. I had this call from a University to study art but I always doubted myself that I would fail the interview as I knew nothing about the French or their tastes. But after we met, I called the university and arranged an interview and guess what?"

"You got through."

"No, I did not. They rejected me. A simple and straight rejection. But it just didn't matter to me anymore. I did not care. I knew I was destined for better things in the field I loved so much."

"And that is music."

"Yes, and that is music. So I came back to the US and just started singing. I would sing at subway stations, I would sing at small gatherings, I would open for unknown bands, but I would sing. And that was what made me happy."

"So you became famous or something?"

"No, not overnight. I told you right. I started off in subways and parties. But I soon had a whole group of people who liked my singing. It just picked from there."

"So why the name change?"

"So that you could not find me. I wanted destiny to make us meet."

She just said that. Said that with such a straight face, not knowing, or not wanting to know, what affect that line had on me. She had changed her name because of me. She had changed her identity so that I could not find her. I was confused. What was this? Why was she so scared if I found out where she was? Was she scared that I would follow her, or was she scared that she was not as strong as she thought she was.

"So I changed my name. And kept it a Shaila. Close enough to a Shalini, but far away from a girl who had lost it all."

"Shalini. But .."

"You know what, it really feels good to hear that name. More so because you are saying it. Over the years I have kind of lost Shalini. I don't know if it is a good thing or bad. I used to be scared and vulnerable, but I had an identity. This new Shaila is kind of a mystery."

"Everything you do is a mystery. Changing your name just like that. That is plain weird."

"I know it is. That is what makes it fun. And I think the name changing is what started the transformation as well. From an under confident Shalini who had lost everything she ever had, to a passionate, fiery, ambitious Shaila, who was willing to do whatever it takes to feed her passion, music."

I did not ask her what 'whatever it takes' implied. I feared the worst, so I just let it hang there as we completed one more round around a huge office building which apparently had parking space for around 2000 cars. Delhi had tried to develop a Manhattan, but in doing so, they had forgotten one small little detail, public transport. Everyone who had to come to office had to drive. The authorities were now looking back at the problem and were trying to build a metro monorail within Gurgaon which had so far only led to more chaos on the roads. I tried to clear my mind and change the question.

"So are you liking India?"

"That's actually a funny question. This is the country where I have spent a major part of my life, in fact, where I had thought I would spend the whole of my life. I thought I would love it. I thought there would be a *Swades* movie type of feel when I get off the plane and I smell the air of Delhi. But honestly, it was just the same. I had thought that there would be people waiting for me in India. The last time when I was at the airport, I was leaving India. There were too many things occupying my mind back then, but this time, I thought it would be special. I thought it would be grand."

"And was it special, was it grand?"

"I don't know about grand, but meeting you certainly has made it special." She smiled at me.

I knew she meant what she had just said. It made me feel good.

When I used to think about Shalini in the last six years, and which was many times, I used to think that I would hit her if she came in front of me. The feeling of hatred was so strong that I was actually willing to hit a girl. But I guess, that was because I had tried to convince myself all these years that I did not care for her. That it did not matter to me that she had left me when I needed her. Yes, that was one thing that she did not realise, at the time we last met, not only did she need me, in fact, I needed her more. I also realised that the feeling of hatred for her had emanated from something else, something which could not make me forget her even though we had only met 3 times before. Was it love? I was not sure. Was it love with Kriti? I was not sure of that either. But one thing I did know for sure was that sitting there, with her, I could be myself without any pretence in the world. And that was a good feeling.

"You know I really hated you for leaving me like that."

"You did?"

"Yes, I hated you for the last six years. I did not know how I would react on seeing you but I was pretty sure it would be violent. But when I saw you today, all the hatred vanished. I don't know why."

She left that hanging in the air and we stalled our walk and sat on a bench in front of the building. Hand in hand, just looking at the offices in front of us. Looking at them, but not seeing them.

"So you always knew that you would see me."

"What?"

"You always knew that you would see me. I mean, you wanted to vent out your anger when you saw me right? So that means that you were pretty sure you would see me."

"I was pretty sure I wanted to see you. What about you? Did you think we would meet again?"

"I did not think, I knew."

We continued looking ahead, hand in hand. I did not want to look at her eyes at that moment, for Kriti's sake.

"So are you like a very big star in US?"

"Not as big as a Lady Gaga or a Britney Spears, mainly because I prefer my pants on than off, but yeah, decently big."

"How big is decently big?"

"If you listen to my agent, he says that I will be signed on by a Cola major to endorse their drink one day, but as of now, if you are a music lover in the US, you would know me."

"I don't really get how big is that, but I assume big enough."

"Haven't you visited US anytime after that?"

"No, I left software and computers after MBA and that is the field in which you really end up in US. Right now I am involved in operations and strategy for an Indian product, so I stay here."

"If I could fake attention, I would ask you more about your work. But I really can't. It seems pretty boring."

"Come on. It's not that boring."

"Can you say that out loud?"

I got up and stood on the bench.

"Yes I can shout it out." I shouted out loud, but I shouted something else

"Why did you never get back in touch?"

I looked at her with all seriousness in my eyes. She pointed me to sit down. I did as I was told. I tried taking her hand again.

"You have lost all privileges to my hand with that stupidity."

She smiled, the smile which reached her eyes. Then she put her head on my shoulder and just lay there for a couple of minutes. And then

"I am sorry. I was only thinking about me. At that time, I was not in a position to think about anyone else. I know I should have. I am sorry. At that time, I needed you more than you needed me. And I was not ready for that."

We sat there for the next fifteen minutes, saying nothing, the moment getting the better of us. Me trying to figure what her last words meant- *I needed you more than you needed me.*

Then she got up. And started walking again. I followed.

"Will you sing for me again?"

"No."

"But why?"

"I sang for you when I had practically stopped singing for the world. That is special. Let it be. I don't want to spoil it."

"I have no answer to that."

I made a sad face.

"Okay, now don't look so distraught. What can I do to make you feel better? Mmmm. Okay, I will talk about your work. So where do you work? In one of these buildings is it?"

"No, my office is close by but not over here."

"You like your work?"

"It pays my bills. I guess that is how much I like it."

"Am sorry, I can't ask you anything more about your work."

I smiled. "As if your work is really interesting."

She raised her eyebrows. "I travel all around the world, meeting all sorts of new people, seeing all sorts of new things, doing what I love to and what I do the best- that is singing. What can be more interesting?"

"Projecting how much your product will sell in the next quarter.

And then multiplying it by 2 to show your seniors that you have a grand vision and being happy for two and a half months in the quarter and taking shit in the last fifteen days. That doesn't sound that bad does it?"

She gave me a disgusted look "Do you even want me to answer that?"

"Not really."

"Thought so."

"So how are your parents?"

"They are good. They are still in the same little town. I have asked them a million times to shift in with me, but they say they can't start their lives all over again."

"Get them."

I saw a tinge of remorse in her eyes.

"If I could have convinced my mom to come with me to the US, maybe she would have been alive today, and maybe, I would have had a family."

"I have tried."

"Try harder."

"So you have no family in India now?"

"No, my parents had no siblings. And my grandparents are also no more. So it is pretty much me alone in this world right now. There are some distant cousins, but we don't even exchange Christmas cards."

"In India, it's Diwali greetings."

"What?"

"In India the phrase is not 'Christmas cards', its 'Diwali greetings'."

"Yeah whatever. I want to eat aaloo paranthas. Can you take me to someplace where we can get those?"

"Yeah whatever."

"Shut up. You can so not pull off a 'yeah whatever.'"

"I so can."

"Can't."

"Do you want aaloo paranthas?"

"Yeah, whatever. See, that's how you use the phrase. Now take me to the aaloo paranthas place."

I really could not pull it off.

"Okay, let's go."

I held her hand again and led her to a dhaba which was an all nighter. My office was not in this area but I had frequented the parantha shop in the vicinity. She would raise some eyebrows considering the time and considering Gurgaon, but I assumed there would be some female population in the form of call centre executives. Luckily, I was right, there were some females around when we got to the place. We sat on one of the corners, as far away from a group of rowdy drunk guys. I could remember more than one occasion when I was one of the rowdy drunk guys and people with females used to sit far away from me. In fact, the only time I had come here with a female was when I had come here with Pooja and when she had decided that we were together. Not a really nice memory. But it had been quite a while.

"What are you thinking?"

"Some old memories of this place. How things change."

"Things change, people should not."

"You changed. In fact, you changed so much that you even changed your name!"

"I am different. Different rules apply to me."

"Oh come on!"

"Yeah, whatever."

She giggled. I giggled right back at her.

"You giggle like a girl."

I giggled some more. The waiter came to take our order.

"So what will you have?"

"I told you right. Aaloo paratha."

"Okay, chill. Anything else?"

She talked to the waiter.

"*Bhaiya, do aaloo paratha with butter ke saath and sir ke liye ek chai and ek aur aaloo paratha.*"

I laughed out. The waiter joined in.

"What?"

"You talk like a Punjabi girl who has lived in Canada too long."

"Oh shut up!"

"Yeah whatever."

I took out my tongue to tease her, the waiter interrupted, surprisingly in English.

"Sir, when you two are done, please call me. I have other work also."

We both looked at him surprised. Me because he spoke English, and she because of his attitude. Before she could say anything, I ordered.

"Three aaloo paranthas, one chai and one Thums Up."

"Fifteen minutes."

"A little quickly please."

"You have a train to catch?"

"No,"

"Then fifteen minutes."

He left. We both laughed. I don't know at what, but we did. He got us the food in less than the stipulated time and we started gorging on the food. It was really good and worth the insult by the hands of the waiter in front of Shalini.

"You know what, now I am getting that Swades movie feeling."

"Is that music playing in the background? Tae tae tae taeeeeee."

"Stop it, you are really bad at it. And yes it is. And even Shah Rukh is there. And he looks so good. And plus, he is not even insulted by the waiter at a dhaba."

"Hold on, he will be in some time."

"Shut up."

I did. She fantasised about Shah Rukh and I just ate the paranthas.

"These parathas are heavenly. I wish you could get something like this in US."

"So how long are you here?"

"Don't worry, this time I will not just run away. Honestly, I am too famous now to run away."

"And pretty modest too!"

"I call a spade a spade."

"But seriously, how long are you here?"

"Long enough."

"Will I get to know how long?"

"What do you think?"

"I think- no."

"Correct answer. But this time, I won't vanish."

"Yeah, considering how famous you are."

"Or considering, that I don't want to."

She looked at me and for the first time, I saw something more than mystery in her eyes. She had always been a mystery to me, but for the first time, I thought that this was leading to something. I did not know yet what it was though.

We ate the paranthas, I paid the guy, no tip of course, and we headed towards nowhere and got close to the national highway.

"You know, there is supposed to be a 15% tip."

"Welcome to India. Here, we do not tip, we ask for a discount."

"Where does this road lead to?"

"Jaipur, if you go like a really long way on it. Otherwise there is Manesar, Pataudi and lots of other small towns."

"You been to any of those places?"

"Yeah, for work."

"Okay, so let's not talk about that. Your work is boring. I like this highway, pretty much like an American highway."

"Yeah, took a long time to build. You see that building over there?"

"Yes, what about it?"

"Well, never mind."

"Tell me."

"Never mind."

"Tell me now."

"You will find it boring."

"Is that your office?"

"Yes, how did you guess?" "Two things, one of course when you said that I will find it boring. And two, the dread in your eyes when you looked at it. Let's go."

"Where?"

"I want to see where you sit."

"Its 3 am at night. It would be closed."

"We will break in."

"I will get fired."

"Come on, we will not steal anything. We will just go inside, take a walk, and come out. Does it have CCTVs?"

"I don't know."

"Then let's check. Come on, don't be a sissy. Plus, if they fire you, your next job will be much better than this."

"How do you know?"

"Because there can be nothing more boring than what you do. Now come on."

So we walked the200 metres to my office. The guy at the security was sleeping so we directly walked into the compound. The same compound which used to be full of people dressed formally in pants and shirts and talking about sales, numbers, promotions and affairs now bore an empty look. There was not a single soul in the vicinity. We tried the door. It was locked. Shalini looked at me and asked me where the fire escape was. I just stood there. She went around the building and found it.

"You are being a chicken."

"I am not chicken. I just don't want to be fired."

"Don't worry, even if you are, I will make you a singer in my troupe. Then atleast life will be a bit interesting."

We entered the fire escape.

"Which floor you sit on?"

"First."

We climbed up to my office. The door was locked. She tried pushing it open. I took out my access card and opened it. She smiled, and we were inside. My office had the typical office look. Some lights were on so that it was not completely dark. There was a huge open space which had cubicles in it, and on the left, right, front and back, there were offices of the senior people, and there were a couple of conference rooms.

"Which office is yours?"

"I don't have an office." And then as an after affect "yet."

I held her hand and took her to my cubicle.

"This is where I sit. A 4 by 4. Now you can go ahead and make fun of it."

Surprisingly, she did not. She sat on my seat and looked at the partitions which separated my cubicle from other cubicles. There were photos of me and Hari at a cricket match, there was a cricket ball signed by Sachin himself, there were one or two certificates from work, and there was a lot of mess. She was taking a very keen interest in whatever was there. She took a couple of minutes studying the photographs, and a couple of minutes making sense of the mess. I sat on my table and she on my chair. There was an eerie and romantic feel about it.

"Have you ever made out with a girl in your office?"

"No."

"That status is not going to change. Now let's go or else you might get caught."

We took the same route to get out of the office and once we were on the highway again, she spoke.

"Thank you."

"For what?"

"For taking me to your office."

And that too, just hung in the air. We walked along the highway for some more time, clueless to where we were going, clueless to where we wanted to go. Just walked. It had been a very long time since I had just walked and doing that with her felt amazing. I thought of Kriti when I was with Shalini. Would I feel the same way had I been walking with her instead of Shalini. I tried to kick the thought out of my mind. Kriti was for real, Shalini was an unknown fantasy. I spoke to clear my head.

"So how long are you here this time?"

She smiled.

"You can ask as many times as you want, but do you really think I will tell you that?"

I let that pass.

"Doesn't this look pretty."

I pointed to the road in the front. It had a hazy look to it. She all of a sudden turned towards me and said

"Kiss me now."

"What?"

"Now."

I puckered my lips and she burst out laughing.

"I got you again with this one."

We both smiled at each other. She spoke

"How desperate are you? Not getting any action is it? Are you seeing someone?"

This was the first time either one of us had asked such a direct question, and she let it slip in so casually. I prepared myself for the answer. I put my hand in my pocket, held the ring and spoke

"I was seeing someone, but it's now over. Been quite some time."

I kept on playing with the ring. I wanted to see her reaction to my statement. Would she be happy that I said I was single? Or would she not really care. She took the latter option. No change of reaction. Nothing at all. And then after 5 seconds, I saw a twitch. I did not know what to make of that.

"Did it hurt?"

"What?"

"The break up?"

"What break up? Oh that, yes it did. I would be lying if I said it didn't hurt. It hurt bad. But it has been more than 8 months now. So I am over it."

I lied to her. There had been no break up. I had been engaged the same day. What was I doing?

"Enough of me. You tell me, are you seeing anyone?"

"No. I waited to meet you again, because I really liked you. But then, I guess I left too much on fate. Should have tried harder to get you. And I liked you all these years, so I really couldn't get into a relationship with anyone else."

I waited, for her to burst into laughter again. I was not going to fall for this any more. But 10 seconds passed, then 20, then a whole minute, and nothing happened. Then she spoke again.

"And I also know you are engaged. I changed my name, you did not. I guess almost the whole world on Facebook knows that you are engaged. You have quite a thing there- Kriti right?"

I didn't know what to say but a yes.

"She is pretty. Very pretty. And you both will look great together. She will make up for your lack in the looks department. And why did you lie to me? You could have told me that you are engaged."

She looked at me expecting an answer. I was not really sure on what was happening.

"I just did not know what to say. We were meeting after all these years. And it was you! I mean, it was you, how could I say that I was engaged. How could I just let you out of my life like that?"

"Well you did by getting engaged."

"But I didn't know that I would see you again. And that too today!" and then as an afterthought. "Is this meeting planned?"

"What do you think?"

"I really don't know what to think. I mean, you have been following me! For how many years? And why did we meet today of all these days? Seems like too much of a coincidence."

"Why do you think? You got engaged today. Today is the last chance I have with you."

"Shalini, I am seriously very confused. Could you please spell it out to me. And yesterday was the last chance you had with me, not today."

"I had to do it sometime, and tonight is as good as any other. So why not."

She held my hand, we stopped walking. She led me to a grass embankment close to the road under a lamp and sat on a bench. She folded her feet and sat facing me, I did the same. This was going to be difficult for her. But I was listening. This could change everything.

"I fell in love with you. It wasn't love at first, but it was love every time after that. And I was so stupid that I could not understand it for so many years."

"When did this happen? On the train."

She broke into a smile. I really wanted to see that smile. Serious talk was on, I wanted something to relax us both. Her smile did it.

"No you idiot. I was too young at that time to love you. I liked you at that time. I told you right, it wasn't love at first. But you were the first guy I ever wanted to talk to."

"So the next time we met? At my college?"

"I guess it was that time. In fact, I am sure it was then. It's not that you looked great or had a great personality or that you were very funny that you swept me off my feet..."

"Thanks. Compliment it is."

"Anytime! Anyways. It was not that you looked great or had a great personality or were very funny..."

"Thanks again."

"Anytime! So, as I was saying, you were not smart, neither were you too funny, but there was something about you. I don't know what it was. I still don't know what it is. In fact, I don't think it's anything about you. It's just the way I feel when I am with you. Its different, it's never been this way with anyone. I just don't want the time to end. "

"But you are the one who has always left without any warning!"

"I know. Because I was scared. Scared of getting you and then of losing you. When we met during college, I was so devoted to my music that I saw you as a big distraction. And when I did not win the competition in your college, I was sure you were a distraction. That was the first time I had ever lost a singing competition. And because I was thinking of you the whole time!"

"Thank you."

"No, I am not putting the blame on you. What I am saying is that you were a distraction."

"No, the 'thank you' was not sarcastic. It was a genuine 'thank you' for thinking about me the whole time. And if it helps, I was thinking of you not only that day, but on many days that followed."

"Obviously you were."

"What is so obvious in that?"

"I told you right. You did not look great, did not have any personality and were not funny. If a girl spent the whole night with you, you ought to be thinking about her for atleast seven years!"

"So that is the reason we met after seven years?"

"Shut up. So as I was saying. I considered you to be a distraction, and hence I did not do anything about us. In fact, as soon as the competition got over, I decided to leave. I knew that had I spent any more time with you, something would have happened."

"You would have fallen for the charm."

"Don't overdo it. So yes, I also thought about you for a long time after that. In fact, for seven years. I always thought that what would have happened had we been together. Would the pain of my father's death been lesser? Would I have been more successful with my music? Would I have been happy?"

Her eyes had lost all color. She was back in the mode she had been seven years ago. She continued.

"Life really did change in those seven years. My father died, my mother died, I failed in the one only thing I thought I could do, I shifted countries to run away from the pain and from a lot many more things and I lost all hope and all confidence in life."

She was quiet, and then she spoke "I will tell you something that I have not told anyone."

There was a pause. I knew this was going to be something big, I just knew it.

"I killed my father."

I did not react. I just kept on looking at her. No reaction. I did not want to judge her, I wanted to understand her.

"I killed my father, with these very hands."

She lifted her hands in despair. This was the first time she had told this to anybody, in fact, I think this was the first time she had said this out loud, she needed time to recuperate. I waited.

"I killed my father with these very hands. He was not a good man, my father. He never loved me or my mother but we made peace with it. He frequented brothels, tried to have affairs, but we made peace with it all. You know, traditional Indian woman would never go against her husband even if he was a fucking man whore. But then, the beating started. When I was around 19, he would come home everyday, and would start beating my mother. I wanted to goto the police, protect her, protect myself, but my mother did not let me. We slowly started making peace with that as well. But then, one day, my mother lost it. My father was dead drunk when he came back home and the usual beating started, but then he did something he had never done before, he hit me. "

"He hit me with a bottle and I started bleeding. My mother lost it after that. She was a devoted Indian wife, but before that, she was an Indian mother. She slapped my father."

There was silence for a minute. Her eyes closed. I knew this was very hard on her. I did not press.

"My father went berserk after that. He slapped my mother, kicked her, did everything possible and I just lay there crying. He kicked her till she was almost dead and then all of a sudden, I got up, took the bottle which he had used, and put it right through him. To end it once and for all."

More silence.

"I went to my mother and we both cried, cried the whole night. But morning came, and we had to do something, and do it fast. She decided to send me to some other country so that I would not be involved in the legal cases. I never regret killing my father, but every living second I regret leaving my mother all alone to fight the battle. I wished I had done things differently, but I was very young at that time, and very frightened. My mother's cousin brother, the same uncle who had picked me at your college, used to send people to US on a fake visa. He had a whole illegal thing going and he knew people who would take care of me in US. So I left my little town, that very morning, never to come back again. The police case about my father's death had escalated and had I been in the country, they might have held me as well. So my mother ensured that my passport was never with me and that I never could come back. In fact, I got to know about her death two months after it actually happened. My uncle was too protective to tell me what had happened. My mother killed herself by hanging from a rope in the mental institution. I guess the guilt of not being a good Indian wife got to her."

I just looked at her, and she just looked at me. She spoke again.

"This is the first time in over ten years that I have come to India. And yes, it does feel nice. The police case got settled soon after, but there was nothing which would bring me back. I had no one here, I had no one there. I was a lost soul. And that is the time I met you in US."

I knew this was the first time she had ever told anyone about this. But she had no tears in her eyes, no emotions in her voice. Just a plain cold look. And it stayed that way for more than five minutes. I wanted to hold her, to console her. But I knew, that she did not tell me this because she wanted consolation, she told me this because she wanted to. It was a burden on her soul and baring herself in front of me the way she had, made her feel better. I just sat with her, letting the past get out of her, get out of her for good.

She spoke again. But this time, there was a spark in her eyes. And the tone was completely changed.

"During those days I thought about you a lot. In fact, you were the only source of hope in my life. I had tried to get back to music, but I had failed in it. I could not understand how two meetings with one person can make you love them so much. But it had happened. I was madly in love with you, and I guess the hope to see you again kept me going on some level. I had left it to fate. After it had been so unfair to me, it had to make me meet you again."

"And it did."

"Yes it did. But the timing was terrible. At that time, I was personally at my lowest. I was getting used to the fact that I had killed my father, and used to the fact that I had deserted my mother. And that is when I met you. And you made a difference."

"I am glad I could help."

"You know, it was not that something happened the day I saw you. It was just that I had met someone I knew after ages. There was a connection with you, you reminded me of my childhood, of my dreams, of music, of love. But I ran away from it all. After seeing what all I had in my life, I thought that you would come, and then just leave. Like everything else."

"What happened then?"

"Then I knew that fate would make us meet again. So honestly, I wanted to make myself worthy of you so that the next time we would meet, I could stand up and say that I love you. As I said earlier, at that time, I needed you more than you needed me. And I did not want it that way. You may think that it is all crap but seriously, I needed something to go on in life. You made me reconnect with myself."

"So this meeting, as you said is not by fate."

"No, I think I trusted fate a little too much to meet you. With the advent of social media, facebook, etc, it is not difficult to find a person with a name as weird as yours."

"Come on, it's not that weird."

"I thank God every day that it is. I had left it all on fate till about a week ago. And then I thought that I had had enough. I found you and came to know you are getting engaged. So here I am, purposely a day after your engagement, to say thank you . And...."

"And what?"

"And to tell you that I love you."

We sat there, looking into each other's eyes. And I knew she meant every word she had just said.

"I really don't know what to do."

"Neither do I. But I feel great that I have told you. In fact, I feel great that finally I have talked about my past."

We both sat on the bench and stared into the dark sky. She then got up.

"I should leave now."

"Where to?"

"I don't know. I thought that I will not run away from you this time. That this time, I will make sure that we are together. But I don't think I can do that. I am just happy that I told you. But I guess it is too late."

"I really don't know what to say. Maybe it is too late. I really like Kriti."

"Just what I thought."

She smiled. If there ever was a fake smile, that was it.

"A little too late. What would have happened had we met yesterday. I had initially thought of meeting you yesterday. Would that have changed your decision?"

"I guess we will never know."

I did not want to break her heart. But I really had no option. She gave me the fake smile again, picked herself up, and left. And left me behind, staring at her, and thinking what could have been.

I woke up to a morning sun, birds chirping in my ears, people jogging around me to stay fit, and old people laughing out loud in unison to stay mentally stable. My eyes opened partly, the sun rays rushing in, and then closed again. Was I living a dream? Had I actually spent the night at a park right next to national highway the day I had got engaged? Startled I sat up and looked around for the comfort of my bedroom. I searched by pocket for my phone. It was 6:45 am. 4 missed calls from Kriti, I could handle that. I could lie that I had too much to drink and lost all senses and crashed at Hari's place. I always had an alibi in Hari. I didn't really know what to do. My head was spinning, I was kind of hungry, and the thoughts of Shalini had started making appearances in my head again. I closed my eyes, took out my handkerchief and put it over my eyes, and lay down to sleep again.

I woke up after 2 hours, still on the very same garden. The sun was out in full force now, the people who were jogging in the morning could now be seen running after busses on the highway, the chirping birds had been replaced by barking dogs in search of food, and the old people were back to sleep. I checked my phone, 7 missed calls, all Kriti. I kept my phone in my pocket, got up and reached out to the highway for a taxi. A taxi stopped, I got on, and he started. He asked me where I wanted to go and I told him to take me towards Delhi.

The phone rang again. It was Kriti again. This time, I picked it up.

"Where have you been? I have been calling you since morning.

How much did you drink yesterday? I even tried calling Hari but even his phone was switched off."

I cursed Hari. He should have taken more care. But Kriti's tone right now was more of concern than of nagging. The nagging would start once we got married I thought.

"I met an old friend, and got talking."

"Oh! Who was the old friend? Some one I would know?"

The tone was now inquisitive, still not nagging.

"No, I don't think you would."

"Hmm, would you care to tell. Male or female?"

I thought she would be a little more subtle in asking, but she wasn't.

"Female. Her name was Shalini."

Kriti hung up. No shouting, just hung up. The cab driver asked me where I wanted to go. I just asked him to go straight, we were crossing Delhi and were taking the Grand Trunk Road which leads to Chandigarh. The phone rang again. It was Kriti.

"Did you spend the night with her?"

"I did. But nothing of the sort what you think happened. We just talked."

"And where did you sleep?"

"In a park."

I don't know why, but I just didn't feel like lying. I could have easily told her that I was with Hari, we had too much to drink, and then slept off. No more questions would have been asked. But I just kept on telling her things that would make her mad.

"In a park? Are you crazy? Did she sleep with you in the park?" and then as an afterthought "Are you crazy?"

"No, she left around 3, I just didn't feel like coming back home so I slept there."

Kriti hung up again, not to call back. The cab driver asked me where I wanted to go. I closed my eyes and tried to relive the last night. I asked him to go straight. Myriad thoughts were going through my mind. Thoughts concerning me, concerning Kriti, concerning Shalini. Was I doing the right thing marrying Kriti when I knew that Shalini could be mine? Did I really want Shalini to be mine- after all how much did I know her. Was it true whatever Shalini had told me yesterday night? Did she really love me? Did Kriti really love me or was she marrying me for a secure future? Did I really love Kriti or was I marrying her for a lack of effort to find someone else? Did I love Shalini or was it the mystery in her which had attracted me to her?

My head started spinning again and I closed my eyes and tried to sleep, but sleep never comes at the time you really want it to. I continued to stare outside. We had left the city now and were in hinterland India. Everything all of a sudden seemed so beautiful, the crops growing in the fields, the woman with earthen pots filled with water on their head, the buffaloes and cows grazing under the trees, small kids running after even smaller dogs, overcrowded jeeps and buses.

All these things, which had seemed irrelevant and redundant till yesterday, now seemed so beautiful and serene. I looked at the rearview mirror. There was a smile on my face, a smile which I had not seen for a long time, a smile which was definitely not there when I woke up for gym every morning, which was definitely not there when I was having Italian food or shopping, a smile which was definitely not there when I was talking to Kriti, a smile which was definitely not there when I was getting engaged.

I checked my pocket and found the engagement ring. I took it out, opened the window, and threw it away.

Just like that.

I noticed the smile, it had not gone away, it had just widened. The taxi driver again asked me where I wanted to go. This time I said Ambala, my hometown.

The taxi continued on its journey towards Ambala. I had to find Shalini. I could not let her go away like the times I had let her go earlier. The first time we had met at the railway station, was at my hometown Ambala. I knew, that after coming back to India after so many years, and after opening up about her past to me yesterday, she would go back to kill the demons which still lived in her head. There were no direct trains from her hometown to Delhi, that is why we had met in the first place, because her family was taking a connecting train to Delhi from Ambala. I hoped that there would still not be any direct trains and she would have to get off at Ambala.

And that is where I would find her.

After thinking of Shalini for some time, the thought of Kriti came to my mind. I never had loved her, but I did care for her. I guess the words I had said during our engagement were a testimony to that. I knew I was doing a terrible thing to her. I knew I could never make up for it, but it was my happiness over hers. And I was selfish.

I guess everyone is. But at that time, I felt it was Shalini's happiness over Kriti's. And I went for Shalini. I knew Kriti would not forgive me, I just hoped she would forget.

The journey towards my hometown continued and as we got near, the anxiety grew even more. In a short while I was there. The taxi dropped me at the railway station. I had old memories of this small city and I occupied a bench amidst all the frenzy in the railway station.

I kept on looking at people as they came and went. Hope in my eyes. Hours passed by, but I knew that I would see her again. Fate could not be so unkind to me. And then after around five hours, a lonely figure came walking around the platform.

She was in a dark green dress. She was fair, had a dimpled chin which gave a something special to her smile, long eyelashes, curly at the end, like a princess would want them, kajal around her eyes, kajal to keep away the bad omen from her beautiful face, a small parrot nose, which twitched when she frowned, and black flowing hair, which I would later know, she thought were brown.

It was Shalini.

She looked at me, our eyes met, and I could see a tear roll down her cheek. I guess she knew why I was there.

"You came."

She ran towards me and we hugged.

"I love you Shalini, I love your beautiful eyes, your dimpled chin, you parrot nose, you black hair. I love you."

She had tears in her eyes but still managed to say "My hair are brown, not black."

ONE YEAR LATER

Hari

Hari was now the proud father of three children. His wife thought that their son was getting bored alone so they needed another kid.

They had twins.

Hari, I think has grown up now.

Pooja and Rannvijay

I did not talk to Pooja after she had dumped me for her ex. But after meeting Shalini, I understood what she did. We are not best friends now but we do exchange Christmas (Diwali) greetings.

Kriti

Kriti has not forgiven me, but I do hope she has forgotten me. We

203

are not in touch but I do get to hear about her from some friends. She is not married yet but I hope she finds someone.

And I hope someday she forgives me for what I did.

My parents

My parents are still based in Ambala and even after infinite requests to move in with us, they continue to stay there. We once took a two week break and lived with them in Ambala the entire duration. I have not seen them as happy as they were in those two weeks for quite some time.

Shalini and I

Shalini now divides her time between me and her music. She is going to release her first album very soon in India and as a tribute to us, has named it 'Seven years.'

Well, for me, life turned out pretty much the way I wanted it. Nice job, nice house, nice car and a wonderful wife.

The car can still be bigger though.